MW00617057

DEATH in the SAUNA

DENNIS ALTMAN

Also by Dennis Altman

DEATH in the SAUNA

DENNIS ALTMAN

Clouds of Magellan Press | Melbourne

First published in Australia in 2023

Clouds of Magellan Press, Melbourne
www.cloudsofmagellanpress.net

Copyright © Dennis Altman 2023

Distributed in Australia by John Reed Books and eBook Alchemy
www.johnreedbooks.com.au
www.ebookalchemy.com.au

ISBN: 978-0-6457328-0-1 (pbk)
ISBN: 978-0-6457328-1-8 (eBook)

Cover design and author photo by Gordon Thompson
Cover image, Victor Furtuna, Unsplash

CRIME FICTION

For Tom Tanhchareun, with whom this story was invented during many lockdown walks in Melbourne 2021

1

Had a different attendant been on duty that night the body might not have been discovered until the morning. But Winston was scrupulous when cleaning out the cubicles, and not willing to ignore one, even if the occupant was sleeping.

Or, as it turned out, dead. After shaking the body a few times without response Winston felt for a pulse, then pushed hard on the bare chest seeking a reaction. None coming he dropped his mop and bucket and rushed downstairs for help, not before checking the cubicle for any signs that might identify the man. Other than a locker key the room was bare.

Luckily Joe Tripaldi the owner was still at the front desk, chatting with the doorman as he counted the night's takings. He followed Winston upstairs, took a quick look at the body, then a longer glance at the face, strangely serene, one hand still clutching a half empty amyl bottle. The corridor seemed deserted, no sign that anyone else had been in the cubicle.

'Ah,' said Joe. 'Well, let me handle this.' He grabbed Winston by the elbow and pushed him out into the half dark corridor. 'Mate,' he said, 'take the night off.' He felt in his pockets, took out two ten-pound notes. 'Not a word to anyone mind,' squeezing Winston's elbow tight. 'I'll make a couple of phone calls … no need to upset the punters.'

Joe carefully shut the cubicle door and looked for an 'out of service' sign to hang on the entrance. Downstairs, in the small room next to the washing machines, which served as his office, he picked up the phone. 'Spencer, I know it's late,' he said, 'but I need you here.'

Twenty minutes later a flustered Spencer Carson, dressed in casual clothes with an unseasonal scarf and cap, tapped at the back entrance to the sauna which gave access to Joe's office. By now the sauna was half empty, and the two of them avoided too many curious stares as they went upstairs and entered the dead man's cubicle, Spencer grimacing at the stale smells in the corridor.

A quick glance confirmed the man was dead, no visible signs of violence, thought Spencer, quickly checking for any tell-tale signs in the cubicle.

'Yes,' he said. 'It's him. Pomfrey Lister.'

'I didn't call the police,' said Joe, as if the thought had occurred to him. 'Seemed better to handle it quietly.' There were, of course, protocols to deal with such an event, but none of them covered the possibility of a high-profile corpse, and someone who might cause problems for the business. Joe had a deeply ingrained suspicion of authority and reporting such a death might lead to too many unwelcome questions. What if Pomfrey had chosen the sauna to commit suicide?

'An accident,' said Joe firmly. 'Maybe too much excitement.' He pointed at the amyl flask. 'Or an overdose.'

Spencer pondered; of course, the death should be reported. But that would lead to considerable publicity for both the sauna and the forthcoming Global AIDS Conference for which he and Pomfrey were jointly responsible. It had already been postponed because of the turmoil that followed the attacks of September 11; two years later anything that disturbed the preparations was to be avoided. 'And,' he said, as if that was his only concern, 'it would bring unnecessary distress to his wife. No, we can manage this ourselves. When does the sauna close?'

'Not for a few hours,' said Joe. 'But we could get everyone out with a fire alarm … clear the place enough to take out the body … if we had somewhere to take it.'

'I think,' said Spencer carefully, 'that both Pomfrey and Mary would prefer that he died at home. In his bed—sudden heart attack perhaps.' He looked at the body, which showed no visible sign of having been attacked. 'Yes.' he said, 'after all that's probably what happened. We just need to make certain—er—locational adjustments. Let me call Mary.'

He ushered Joe into the corridor, taking out a new model Blackberry. 'Mary,' he said, 'we have a problem. Prepare yourself for a shock. Pomfrey is dead.'

A gasp at the other end of the phone, as Mary felt for a chair. 'Yes,' said Spencer, 'now this is what I want you to do.' He checked that Joe was not listening. 'We will bring the body to your house. I'll explain when we get there. Stay calm and do exactly as I tell you. We'll need a doctor to confirm his death—someone we can trust.'

Mary gulped. 'Should I call our GP?'

'No,' said Spencer. 'Better not. Do you know Alejandro Herrera? Call him and tell him that Pomfrey has had a sudden heart attack and you can't contact your regular doctor. You know Alejandro, right?'

'I think so,' said Mary. 'Pomfrey's colleague?'

'Yes. He can be trusted—' He broke off, as Joe came back into the cubicle. 'Mary,' said Spencer firmly, 'get ready. We can be at your house in half an hour. I'll talk to you again before we get there.'

He sized up Joe, who had the appearance of someone whose gym attendance was still keeping pace with his appetite for rich food. 'Think the two of us might manage? My car is parked right round the back.'

A few minutes later the remaining patrons were startled by the peremptory blast of a siren and an announcement that this was a fire drill, and they should immediately proceed outside. Within twenty minutes thirty men, mainly dressed only in skimpy white towels, gathered uneasily outside in what was, for London, a reasonably balmy night. One man, now clearly able to see the person with whom he had just been intimate, would have fled had he thought to bring his car keys with him in the rush. Spencer caught a glimpse of the clientele and shuddered; his stake in the sauna did not mean, he reassured himself, that he approved of what went on inside.

'I've talked with his wife,' said Spencer, as he and Joe sized up the difficulty of carrying a dead body down the stairs and out through the back exit, kicking aside discarded condom wrappers and marijuana butts on the floor. 'She will back us up.'

Mary, he thought, had been shocked but not surprised to hear of her husband's death, but he was confident she had grasped what needed to be done.

Twenty minutes later, as he and Joe drove across town to Pomfrey's residence, the now restless patrons were re-admitted and promised two free passes to make up for their embarrassment. Meanwhile Winston was quietly getting drunk in a bar that catered for young men looking for possible patrons, and decided he had perhaps imagined the whole thing.

∽

Waiting for the men to arrive seemed endless for Mary. She was upset, but also furious: even before Spencer could confirm it she had a clear idea where Pomfrey had died. Grief, she told herself, could wait; the immediate need was to make Pomfrey's death seem as dignified and natural as possible. He had no public history of heart problems, but he had been working particularly hard in the leadup to the conference, on which he thought rested his best chance of recognition in the next honours list.

Still in shock she found Alejandro's number in the list by the phone and paged him. Pomfrey had clearly died in peculiar circumstances and avoiding the family doctor seemed wise. Alejandro was Pomfrey's collaborator and rival, but he still saw patients in the hospital HIV clinic, and more than anyone he would appreciate the need to prevent scandal tarnishing the upcoming Conference. If it were put to him that Pomfrey had suffered a massive heart attack and was already dead when Mary called, would Alejandro ask too many questions?

Luckily Alejandro was still awake and willing to come round. He could be there in thirty he assured Mary, giving her time to freshen up and change into clothes that seemed more befitting. He arrived surprisingly quickly, if a little dishevelled, a short man verging on plumpness, who projected an air of self-importance, as if he were already preparing his remarks on receiving the next award. He and Pomfrey had been working for some years on finding a vaccine for HIV, well aware that a breakthrough would lead to both fame and money. Alejandro owed his name to a Colombian mother, but he had grown up in the home counties, and spoke with the careful tones of someone who had gone to a private school, if not the best of private schools. He had been driving his new BMW with the roof down, he told Mary proudly, as he carefully removed his leather jacket.

Mary had decided to be frank; she knew Alejandro had mixed feelings about Pomfrey but his concern for the reputation of their joint research would assure his discretion.

'He didn't actually die at home,' she confided. 'And Spencer and a-a colleague—helped bring him back to the house.'

She hoped that Alejandro was sufficiently prudish to not ask too many questions; enough she thought to assure him that while Pomfrey had apparently died of a massive heart attack it would only cause embarrassment and publicity were it to be known he had not died at home.

Alejandro pondered. 'Of course,' he said, stroking his small but neatly trimmed moustache, 'I would need to examine the body.'

'Yes,' said Mary, pouring them both a large whisky. 'I so appreciate—I couldn't stand the scandal if people knew—if they thought Pomfrey was not behaving as he should ...'

She blew her nose vigorously, possibly wiping away a tear, and gave Alejandro her most beseeching look. 'I know,' she said, 'that

Pomfrey always looked on you as a great friend and a great scientist.'

'How was his health in general? Any warning signs.'

Mary pondered. 'You knew he was diabetic, of course? And his GP—he's away at the moment—was concerned about possible hypertension.' She sighed. 'And with the Conference ... he was working so hard. It's all become so much more difficult, hasn't it? Constantly worrying about terrorists and whether the Conference might be targeted.'

A knock on the door. 'Alejandro,' she said, 'maybe you could look through Pomfrey's latest notes for the Conference while we prepare the body.'

She ushered him into a large study, where an open laptop sat on the desk, knowing that might engage Alejandro's attention for long enough to prepare the body for examination.

Pomfrey's body was already beginning to become rigid, and Joe and Spencer struggled to carry it out of the car and up the stairs. They had shrouded it in a couple of towels, which Mary quickly threw into the laundry basket, as the three of them wrestled it into the bed. Spencer took Mary aside for a couple of minutes, talking to her earnestly, then guided her back to the body. She held back sobs as she gently sponged down the face, then, pulling the blankets over his chest she called Alejandro into the room.

'His glasses!' she exclaimed suddenly. 'Where are his glasses?'

But before that could be answered Alejandro had entered. He said hello to Spencer, looked slightly puzzled to see Joe in the room, then leant over the bed.

'Yes,' said Alejandro, giving the body a quick glance. 'Yes. Looks what I'd expected ...'

'Definitely cardiac arrest,' said Spencer. 'He wouldn't even have known.'

Mary gestured at the bottle of statins by the bed. 'He was under a lot of pressure,' she said. 'And not that young anymore.'

Alejandro, who was two years younger, nodded complacently. Luckily he had brought his medical bag, one that he was less and less called upon to use. He gave the body another look, felt for any obvious signs of bruising, then filled out and signed a medical cause of death certificate.

The four of them—Mary; Alejandro; Spencer; Joe—gathered downstairs in the living room. It was now 2.00am and they all desperately wanted to sleep and were equally unwilling to leave. All of them had, they slowly realised, participated in what might be a crime, now they were bound together as accessories.

'Well,' said Mary, fighting off exhaustion, 'things to do.'

'The certificate is here,' said Alejandro. 'You will need to take it to the undertakers.'

'Yes,' said Mary, thinking. 'Cremation. Definitely cremation.'

'The Conference ...' Spencer cleared his throat nervously. 'It opens in three days ... of course we can't rush things ...'

'I know an undertaker,' said Joe. 'My cousins have a business. Unless you already ...?'

'Maybe,' said Spencer, thinking how to turn this to his advantage, 'maybe we could hold a memorial for Pomfrey on the last day of the Conference. That is, Mary, if you are comfortable with the idea.'

An uneasy silence: 'I need to tell his family,' said Mary suddenly. 'But Pomfrey really has no family to speak of. There's his aunt, but she's overseas I think. We always used to say we bonded because neither of us had in-laws to worry about.'

For the first time since hearing the news she wanted to cry as what had happened started to take its toll. She snuffled away a tear and stood up. 'Well,' she said, 'let's be practical.'

This was the woman Spencer knew, the tough campaigner who had founded *God Loves Us All* to work amongst AIDS orphans in Africa, had spent months battling recalcitrant authorities in Kenya and Zambia. Mary was a handsome woman, with a slight resemblance to Judy Dench, and she prided herself, as Spencer well knew, on her practicality.

'I'll call Sylvie in the morning,' she said. 'She'll know who to inform.'

'Sylvie?' Joe looked surprised, but the others knew she had been Pomfrey's chief of staff, almost an extension of him and occasionally a companion when Mary was overseas seeking orphans to rescue. Spencer and Alejandro nodded energetically. Sylvie would, as she had so often in the past, manage.

'Can I call a cab?' said Joe standing.

Mary walked with Joe to the front door.

'I'll empty his locker in the morning,' said Joe quietly, to Mary. 'I can drop his clothes round when it's convenient.'

'Better give them to Spencer. He can bring them over,' she replied.

Alejandro joined them. 'I can give you a lift, Joe,' he said.

Mary watched the two disappear into the night and returned to the living room. 'I need to go to bed,' she declared. She looked at Spencer. 'Can the undertakers come for the body in the morning?'

∞

On the other side of London, in a neat studio in Kennington, Sylvie was lying awake, turning over the latest problems from the Conference. Anyway, she told herself, if one was asleep, one couldn't enjoy the quiet of the dark hours before dawn. An unscheduled hour was a rare thing in the week leading up to the opening.

She was half drifting back to sleep when the phone rang. Sylvie rolled over and picked it up.

'Sylvie, this is Mary Lister.' Mary's voice was trembling in a way Sylvie had never heard before. 'I need your help.'

'What is it, Mary? Is everything okay?'

'He's dead. Pomfrey is dead.'

Sylvie felt both stunned and frantic, trying to make sense of Mary's news. 'But how?' she asked, 'he was fine yesterday.'

Mary filled her in—a sudden heart attack. Before Sylvie could react, Mary continued. 'Sylvie, I know it's barely morning, but could you come over? You're just ... there's nobody else. You were closer to him than anyone else I know.'

'Of course,' Sylvie said automatically. She was already up, sliding into the suit she'd laid out for the coming day. 'I'll be there as soon as I can.'

'Thank you.'

'And Mary,' added Sylvie. 'I'm so very sorry.'

But Mary had already hung up the phone.

ᘓ

On the long underground ride to Highgate, Sylvie found herself caught between disbelief, sadness and irritation: Pomfrey's death jostled with the immediate problems of the imminent Conference. It was still early, and the train was half full of yawning commuters and a couple of sleepy shift workers returning home. Sylvie left the station, crossed Archway Road and walked briskly to the Lister's house.

Forty-seven minutes after leaving home she was inside, placing a cup of tea—English Breakfast, two sugars, milk first— into the shaking hands of a woman she had always thought of as impregnable. Mary Lister: Sylvie had heard some of her colleagues jokingly call her the African Tartar. It wasn't unreasonable, Sylvie thought. The woman had helped thousands of people and probably helped save countless lives through her relentless philanthropy. Sylvie wasn't fully comfortable with the missionary aspect of her charity, with its emphasis on abstinence and prayer, but she respected the work they did with AIDS orphans.

Some years ago, Pomfrey had bought a four-bedroom terrace house in Highgate, close to Queen's Wood, with a southward facing back garden. Sylvie had visited several times and thought the house was rather large for two people, although she assumed they each had their own study. The living room, fronting onto the street, was spotless, with large windows looking out onto the garden, and dominated by two large paintings, which Sylvie recognised as products of New York abstract impressionism, strangely out of keeping with the personalities who lived beneath them. Only a large vase of freshly picked white and blue lilacs, and a few photographs on a sideboard, seemed to suggest anything personal about the inhabitants of the house. Sylvie walked over to Mary, ready to embrace her, but then pulled away. Despite having known Mary for years, despite the time they'd spent together, Sylvie knew the prospect of *touching* Mary Lister was far too intimate for Mary's very British stoicism—even if it was to signal that she shared her grief.

Instead, she sat on the couch opposite Mary and pretended to sip at her tea. 'What on earth happened? Pomfrey seemed fine yesterday.'

Mary shook her head as if confused, but she had rehearsed her story. 'I woke in the middle of the night, and I knew something was wrong. He was so cold. I was going to call an ambulance, but I could tell he was gone already. It looked like heart failure to me, Sylvie. It does happen to men his age.'

'You called an ambulance?'

'There was no point. I called Alejandro—he came at once. And confirmed it was Pomfrey's heart.'

'I can't imagine how you must be feeling, Mary.' Sylvie was starting to feel a headache, brought on by lack of sleep and shock.

'We'll have to get his affairs in order very quickly,' Mary said.

'I can take care of everything to do with the Conference.' Sylvie pulled out her phone and opened her organiser.

'Pomfrey's irreplaceable, obviously, but I've begun with the easy things. I think I have some names in mind for the panels he was due to appear on, and—'

Mary cut her off. 'He needs to be cremated.'

Sylvie blinked. 'Shouldn't we wait for the will?'

'No, I know what Pomfrey wanted. We've been married for twenty-eight years. God knows we'd discussed it enough.'

'All right, I'll deal with the paperwork.' Paperwork was something Sylvie could do.

Mary stood up, walked over to the sideboard, and brought Sylvie a piece of paper. 'You'll need this. It's the cause of death certificate. Alejandro signed it off last night.'

Sylvie took the paper from Mary and noticed Mary's hands weren't shaking anymore. But her own hands were. She had cried briefly when Mary rang her that morning, as shocked by Mary's apparent vulnerability as by the news. She had worked with Pomfrey for three years now, had moved from temporary assistant to invaluable confidante for both Pomfrey's scientific and political work. Perhaps, she thought sadly, she had known a side to him hidden even from Mary; immersed in his work Pomfrey seemed to have had virtually no life beyond the laboratory and the various international meetings that over the past year had taken up more and more of his time as Conference planning progressed. With Mary he seemed to have an almost formal relationship, as if whatever passion had once existed had long ago given way to mutual convenience.

Outsiders wondered whether she and Pomfrey were linked romantically, but that suited them both; Pomfrey, whose private life was carefully barricaded, Sylvie who had a discrete and no longer very satisfying relationship with a married man. She had seen Geoffrey on and off now for several years, but the intervals between meetings were growing, the romantic weekends away, snatched from his family, becoming a memory. The last time they had met he had muttered something about needing to be more careful, and Sylvie realised she was somewhat relieved. She realised how little she really knew about him, even his job—he described himself vaguely as a financial planner—was somewhat mysterious.

'I'll go into the office,' she said. 'Notify everyone. Or do you need me to come with you to the funeral home?'

Mary shook her head. 'No,' she said, 'I've already arranged to go there with Spencer.'

သ

Three days before the Conference was due to begin, thought Sylvie, was an inconvenient time for Pomfrey to die. Holding a major AIDS Conference in London had been a major obsession of his for many years, one where his role as founder and president of the

Global AIDS Trust would be widely recognised.

There were practicalities to be dealt with, not least of which was the opening session at which a minor Royal had been scheduled to appear, along with a former prime minister of the Gambia and the daughter of a famous Hollywood actor who had made AIDS orphans her primary charity. Pomfrey excelled in hosting such guests; would Alejandro be able to manage?

Pomfrey was a world-class virologist but he was also a consummate diplomat who rarely begrudged the time politics took him away from his laboratory. Like Alejandro he was consumed by a search for an HIV vaccine, where they both cooperated and competed, Pomfrey having let on in a moment of indiscretion that he hoped it might win him a Nobel Prize.

Well, that ambition was over, thought Sylvie, and his competitors might be glad. But in the meantime there were considerable loose ends to deal with. Already several thousand delegates had arrived, and preliminary meetings were being organised as spokespeople for those whose voices are ignored competed loudly for attention. The logistics of these meetings were problems for Spencer, as chief executive of the organisation, but Pomfrey was crucial in smoothing over conflicts and reassuring every delegate that theirs was a crucial voice. The afternoon before his death he had presided over the opening of the People's Village where African women sold hand sewn shirts and young men with tattoos handed out free condoms. A small group tried to disrupt one of the pharmaceutical exhibitions, not before taking advantage of the excellent free cappuccinos and biscotti from their stand.

The Conference was accountable to a large number of interlocking committees, representing every group which could claim a stake in the epidemic, but key decisions were made by the quartet: Pomfrey, Alejandro, Spencer and Sylvie. Odd, thought Sylvie, that they were also the only people who already knew of Pomfrey's death, but that also simplified things. It left her with only one other person whom she needed to inform before the inevitable press stories.

2

Noel rolled up the shutters of the shop with a sense of ennui. Business in secondhand books was slow at best and given the weather it was likely to be even slower today. Noel looked at the street outside, already lit by the morning sun, and thought of all the places he'd rather be, starting with that pool on Hampstead Heath where men lay around in briefs signalling their availability.

As he was sorting through a new consignment from a deceased estate, rich in detective stories from the thirties and old railway guides, the phone rang.

'Are you alone?' asked Sylvie.

'Sadly yes,' said Noel, looking at the empty shop.

'I have some bad news.' She paused, not sure how to say it. 'Pomfrey is dead.'

Noel sat back in his chair, trying to take this in. 'No,' he said. 'That can't be—I saw him two nights ago ...'

'He died in his sleep,' said Sylvie. 'Mary called me to the house this morning. Apparently he'd gone to bed early, said he was tired.'

'But—' Noel paused, trying to recall when he had last seen Pomfrey. 'He was healthy ...'

Had it been only last week that he'd teased Pomfrey that for a man of his age he was remarkably priapic. He was proud of the word, which he'd encountered sorting through a box of books that had just come into the store.

'Massive heart failure apparently,' said Sylvie, struggling to stay calm. 'Mary called in Professor Herrera, who confirmed it.'

She paused. 'They've taken the body to the funeral home. Mary insists on a quick cremation. Intimate family only.'

There was a silence, both of them thinking what this might mean.

'Oh,' said Noel, 'so I can't …'

'No,' said Sylvie. 'I'm sorry.'

How much did Sylvie know, wondered Noel. Enough it seemed to ring him; not enough to share his feelings. 'I'm your mistress,' he remembered saying to Pomfrey, rather enjoying the sense of subterfuge. But mistresses, as he sadly recognised, have no right to share in grief. If he were to mourn Pomfrey he would need to do it in private.

Outside two cats stirred in the sun and a woman trundled past, her eyes intent on reading directions on the back of an envelope. No customers seemed likely; he grabbed a bottle of water and his clunky Blackberry and slammed the door behind him, feeling the *Do Not Disturb* sign was an appropriate message for today.

He needed to walk, and without consciously planning it he found himself walking in the direction of the Heath. How much had Pomfrey really meant to him, he wondered, this older man who was so immersed in work that he only saw him once or twice a fortnight.

He'd met Pomfrey online, as he'd met several others over the past few years—when, thought Noel, had he met someone the old-fashioned way, in a bar or perhaps idling on a street corner? Noel had persuaded the shop's owner to invest in an Intel computer, claiming it would allow them to check sales and expand their business, but he soon discovered other uses for the device. The launch of Gaydar a few years earlier had opened up new possibilities, and soon men were cruising each other on desktop computers, sometimes more willing to share images of their genitals than their faces.

All they knew of each other before they met was constrained by small images, in which Pomfrey's face was half-hidden, presumably by design, suggesting an aquiline nose and slightly full lips. Noel's pictures were more informative: his favourite was one of him lying back against the railings of a small yacht, his body angular in the sun. It was enough for Pomfrey to pursue him, sending messages, sometimes several times a day, until Noel agreed to meet.

Pomfrey had chosen a small coffee shop, inconveniently situated off the Edgware Road, hidden in an enclave of Indian and Greek cafés, and Noel took several wrong turns, before finding the almost empty coffee bar. At first it seemed as if there was no-one there who fitted Pomfrey's description, but in a half-concealed booth toward the back he spied a man with a shock of silver hair, dressed in an expensive suit, who was clearly on edge, watching for his arrival. Pomfrey stood up, offering his hand in a strangely formal greeting; Noel's first impression was that he was taller than he'd expected, with thick dark eyebrows, accentuated by clearly expensive horn-rimmed glasses. Noel was suddenly conscious of his own jeans and rather dishevelled sweatshirt, but Pomfrey put him at ease. Almost immediately Noel sensed a contained energy about the man, which lit up his face and made him strangely attractive. Noel was not very ambitious, but he was drawn to ambition in others, and he was ready to bed Pomfrey to explore his energy. It took several meetings to organise their first time together; Noel rented his share of a flat from an older woman who was unsympathetic to casual visitors, and Pomfrey was reluctant to invite him home.

But Mary was away frequently, and after their third meeting Pomfrey booked a room in a nearby hotel, where somewhat to Noel's surprise they spent an exhausting, sexy night together. That was a little over a year ago, and the relationship had continued, meeting up between Pomfrey's frequent travels and work commitments, gradually acknowledging that it was becoming a serious relationship.

Pomfrey remained married, although whatever passion might once have existed between him and Mary had long died. Noel occasionally hooked up with other men, determined to prove to

Pomfrey, even more to himself, that he was not dependent on their relationship. He liked to claim that their relationship was, in the language he now encountered online, one of friends with benefits, but when, some months earlier, Pomfrey suggested they end it he was devastated. Noel was determined to persist and suggested they commit to monogamy. Had he loved him? Was it only now that he was dead that he could accept that, yes, he had? Pomfrey was the first man he'd met who accepted him as he was, hadn't tried to change or improve or educate him, though in fact he did all those things. His death left him feeling both empty and conflicted.

He had already walked a few miles, and now was on that part of the Heath that was rich in bushes and undergrowth. A young man, dressed in skimpy shorts and t-shirt ran past him into the trees and nearby he spotted two guys, maybe in their forties, wearing baseball caps and sunglasses. Was it the shock of unexpected death, thought Noel, that lead him to cruise for instant sex while he was still coming to terms with Pomfrey's death? Freud, he suspected, could explain it.

Noel was about to follow the path into a more shaded area when he was stopped short by a nagging memory. The previous evening he'd been having drinks with a couple of other booksellers. The evening dragged on, ending with him going with one of them, a specialist in vintage physique magazines, to a small bar he knew in Shoreditch where the clientele wore far more leather than seemed called for in July, even in a London summer. Eventually Michael drove him home, and on the way he was almost sure he'd noticed Pomfrey's car. Not that Noel took much notice of cars, but a bright red Bentley was hard to miss and at the time Noel wondered what Pomfrey might be doing in Spitalfields. There was nothing there likely to be of much interest to a man like Pomfrey unless … Noel had little experience of gay saunas, but he remembered there was a famous one maybe a street or so away from where he'd seen the car.

Noel had had too much to drink and thought nothing more of the sighting when he awoke. But if it had been Pomfrey's car was he really at the sauna that night, having told Noel he had too much to do before the Conference and needed an early night? Hadn't Sylvie said he died in bed? But had she said when?

Of course, Noel told himself, he could have been mistaken about the car. Even if he was right, there might be other reasons for Pomfrey to have been there, although after midnight few came to mind. Suddenly Noel lost any interest in hanging around the Heath and decided he needed to go home and think this through. Perhaps, he thought, trudging back down the hill, he might even go to the sauna and ask ...

CB

Back in the office Sylvie started sorting through the pile of incoming messages for Pomfrey, wondering how best to announce his death. As his assistant she had access to his work emails, and she was about to compose a general message when she remembered a folder marked private. She would never have touched it while Pomfrey was alive, but what were the rules now?

Sylvie stood and paced, torn between curiosity and fear that she might discover something best left alone. Unsurprisingly curiosity won; after all, she told herself, there might be something demanding her attention.

Loyally she ignored the few messages that seemed to have come from Noel and looked for others. A couple seemed to represent orders from vaguely described retailers, and there were several messages from someone identified only as Righteous.

Puzzled, Sylvie opened the message exchange: it seemed that Pomfrey was expressing concerns that certain churches in Africa were funding homophobic messages as part of their HIV prevention strategy. The issue had already been raised in the lead-up to the Conference; what surprised Sylvie was the personal tone of these messages, the references to what seemed to be a personal connection between Pomfrey and Righteous. Whoever was writing these demands for a firm stand against sexual debauchery and support of abstinence appeared to be addressing the demands directly to Pomfrey rather than simply to the head of the Trust.

Even more interesting was the reference in several other messages to possible financial irregularities and the potential involvement of the Inland Revenue. Perhaps she should refer these to Spencer, who kept a firm hand on the Trust's finances.

She was still searching for more messages when Noel called. Back in the shop from the Heath he was reliving the day, thinking back over what little Sylvie had told him.

'So,' he said, 'did you say Pomfrey was going to be cremated?'

'Mary said that's what he wanted.'

'It doesn't make sense,' said Noel. 'A while ago a friend of his died and Pomfrey was very upset after the funeral because he had been cremated. Said he hated to see the body just go up in flames, that it was more dignified to bury it.' He paused. 'At least, I think that's what he said.'

'But,' said Sylvie, 'Mary was very positive. And she's set it for day after tomorrow: the morning before the Conference opens.'

'Where?'

Sylvie paused; Mary had been very firm that she wanted as few people there as possible. 'Noel,' she said carefully, 'I don't think you can be there.'

3

The cremation took place on a grey morning in Kensal Green, one of the city's oldest cemeteries and resting place of writers such as Thackeray and Trollope. Because it had been arranged in haste only the larger chapel was available, which just emphasised how few people showed up. Mary, wearing a clearly old if barely worn black bombazine frock, arrived with two older women who were board members of her charity, and took a seat in the front, briefly acknowledging the other mourners, and nodding to the attendant to play the first piece of music, one of Handel's more famous anthems.

One of the women stood and read a short biography of Pomfrey, noting that he was one of the youngest persons ever to be awarded a doctorate in virology by Johns Hopkins University and that he had co-authored over three hundred refereed publications, including many in the *Lancet* and *Nature*. Both Spencer and Alejandro spoke, praising Pomfrey's contribution to virology and public health, but in ways that sounded as if they had hardly known him. The only family present was a cousin, dressed in an ill-fitting dark suit, who spoke of the younger Pomfrey, still a medical student, who had delighted in riding a motor bike and would lead small groups on long expeditions into the countryside.

Mary had not been sure if she would have the composure to speak, but she rose and walked to the front.

'Pomfrey was a remarkable man,' she said, 'as others have already noted. But I knew him as a person, someone who was always dedicated to his work and always loyal to what he believed. Above all, he was a man of integrity. If something wasn't right Pomfrey would not rest until he'd fixed it. He said that was something his parents had taught him, the need to always stand up for what you know is right, even if it's going to hurt you.' Her voice shook a little, but she stayed composed.

'Maybe ours wasn't always the most conventional marriage, but we were always each other's best friend. He was my moral compass, and I shall miss him.'

It all felt, thought Sylvie, so unfinished, as if the ghost of Pomfrey were hovering, needing to tell them something. That only twelve people had shown up seemed wrong, even though Mary had insisted the service be both short and private. Maybe, thought Sylvie, this is what our lives amount to, an impersonal ending in an alien environment, sung into oblivion by the music of the eighteenth century.

The small group of mourners gathered uncomfortably in the garden afterwards, and Mary led Sylvie down a small avenue of poplar trees. 'It's what he would have wanted,' said Mary firmly. 'No fuss.'

'Did you have any idea?' asked Sylvie tentatively. 'Were there any signs that he might have a heart attack?'

Mary sighed. 'Not really,' she said. 'Of course, he was diabetic. And blood pressure—with all the strain of his big research project, the Conference ...'

She looked at Sylvie. 'When the Conference is over,' she said, 'come and talk with me. We need to think about your future.'

Mary had not cried, Sylvie noticed, but was that through lack of grief or an inability to express it? How little we know others, she thought, realising that her own feelings about Pomfrey were ambivalent. She'd worked for him for three years now, but her work had been largely concerned with the AIDS Trust, not his research or other scientific duties. She had been the perfect executive assistant, but at some cost: Pomfrey would call on her on evenings and weekends, once she had given up most of an Easter break to organise flight bookings for the Trust's international advisory board.

Of course, there had been compensations. Twice he'd taken her with him to overseas conferences, in Los Angeles and then Bangkok. When he suggested the first trip she'd wondered whether he was planning to seduce her, but on the contrary: he treated her with studied courtesy and seemed to forget she was there except when he needed someone to take notes and keep track of his schedule. One evening, after a work dinner at a nearby Persian restaurant, she had noticed Pomfrey talking intensely with a much younger, dark-haired boy, and thought nothing of it, but looking back it should have alerted her.

The discovery of his affair with Noel came soon after the Los Angeles trip, when she noticed a series of phone calls for Pomfrey that all came from the same number, a number she didn't recognise. Each time the caller, a man's voice, said he'd call back but left no name. On the fourth try Sylvie lost patience and demanded a name. 'Noel,' said the voice tentatively and hung up. Pomfrey seemed irritated when she told him, and said he wouldn't call again, but two days later a flustered Noel showed up at the office, and in a slightly shaky voice said he needed to see Pomfrey and he would wait as long as he need. Sylvie's first impression of him was a man on the brink of middle age, with thick brown hair and a worried but pleasant face, who might have been conventionally handsome but for eyes set slightly too close together, accentuating a thin but longish nose.

Suddenly Pomfrey appeared in Sylvie's office and beckoned Noel aside. It was clear from their body language that they were arguing, but after a couple of minutes Sylvie noticed that Pomfrey's whole body relaxed, and he grabbed Noel, holding him tight. After another couple of minutes, during which the two men seemed locked together, Noel left, seemingly both relieved and startled.

'There you have it,' said Pomfrey in a flat tone to Sylvie. 'I love that man.'

They never discussed it again, but some weeks later Sylvie, having spent an hour or so browsing the Camden Markets, wandered into the secondhand bookshop where Noel was seated behind the counter. She recognised him instantly, the slender youngish looking man with a shock of unruly brown hair and a slightly troubled look, as if on guard for anything unexpected. She was tempted to leave, but then he looked up from the counter and smiled tentatively at her, not sure whether they knew each other.

'Noel,' she said, 'I met you—that is, I work for Pomfrey.'

Noel looked at her, his eyes flickering. 'Has he sent you—?'

'No,' said Sylvie quickly. 'He has no idea—*I* had no idea you worked here.'

'It's not my shop,' said Noel apologetically. 'But Mrs Mackie is old now, she lets me manage things. Are you looking for a book?'

'Not really.' Sylvie laughed, slightly self-conscious. Actually,' she said, 'I collect Agatha Christie paperbacks. More for the covers than anything else.'

'Ooh,' said Noel enthusiastically, 'Let's see what we have.' He walked to the back of the store and retrieved a handful of slightly worn paperbacks. 'You want older ones, right? The ones with garish covers? There are two here.'

He placed two old Great Pan books on the counter, both with the title *The Secret of Chimneys*, one with a woman's face, her lips and fingernails painfully scarlet, the other with an equally red hand looming over a gun atop a pile of letters. 'Both published in 1956,' he said, looking inside, 'but with different covers.'

'I love them,' said Sylvie. 'It's one of her silliest—international jewels and fictitious Eastern European monarchies—I've never seen those editions.'

'I could let you have them both,' said Noel calculating, 'for ten quid. They'd be collectibles if they were in better condition.' He looked a little sheepish. 'I've never read her,' he said. 'I have seen a couple of the movies though.

'Do you often get original paperbacks in stock?'

'Sometimes. Mrs Mackie used to ferret around in junk shops for them.' He grinned. 'Come back next week,' he said. 'I'll see what I can lay my hands on. And you can educate me in the world of Agatha Christie.'

Sylvie smiled. 'I think,' she said deliberately, 'you want to ask me about Pomfrey, not Agatha.'

But ten days later she came back, and Noel proudly showed her the latest acquisition, an American paperback with the title *Poirot Loses a Client*, a curvaceous brunette in a pool of blood on the cover, which proclaimed: *The Lady's Plea For Help Was Heard 59 Days After Her Murder*. Sylvie seized it with glee; she had only seen a couple of the old Avon paperbacks.

'Next time,' she promised, 'I'll take you for coffee', scribbling her phone number on a card for Noel, but before there could be a next time Pomfrey died.

❧

The opening night of the Conference saw a party at the sauna. Maybe eighty or so of the delegates, some of them still carrying the Conference bags, emblazoned with the logos of half a dozen drug companies, turned up, casting furtive glances to see who else might be there. A couple of veteran Conference goers had a quiet word at the front desk and arranged to have the proceedings televised into the small lounge that acted as a rest stop for men tired of the sexual activity elsewhere.

Noel came out of the tube and walked up Bishopsgate towards Shoreditch. It took him a few minutes to find the sauna, which sat behind an enormous warehouse in a small back street, almost a lane, strangely deserted although it was only a few minutes away from the markets. Noel hadn't realised that his visit coincided with Conference night and wasn't prepared for the line of men waiting to enter. Nervously he turned away and walked down the street, thinking he couldn't go through with it.

He was halfway to Liverpool Station when he stopped, turned abruptly and returned. At the entrance a bored teller took down his details and issued him with a towel and a locker key, buzzing the lock to let him in. Noel stumbled over a step and entered a long narrow locker room, where half a dozen men were undressing, carefully avoiding any form of eye contact. Noel noted that after stripping down they each wrapped the flimsy white towel around their hips, and several took flip-flops out of their locker to protect their feet.

Appropriately wrapped, Noel followed several men to another set of stairs which led up to a large, enclosed space containing a small swimming pool, a few plastic deck chairs, and on one wall a gigantic mural, depicting what he assumed was meant to be a Roman bathhouse. He was struck by the total absence of windows; once inside the venue it was as if he had left the world behind, the whole place bathed in a dim artificial light which gave everything a slightly bluish tinge.

OK, thought Noel, but whom do I ask. He tried to retrace his steps to the entry desk, took a wrong turn and found himself in a dimly lit corridor lined with small cubicles. The sounds of passion, or at least sexual effort, came from behind several closed doors.

A hand grabbed his left shoulder and pulled him round: 'Hello stranger,' said Michael, his physique magazine friend. 'Thought you never came to places like this.'

Noel explained; maybe Michael could help. As he'd expected the sauna might keep records of who entered, but they would hardly share them with a stranger. 'Your best bet,' said Michael, 'is one of the masseurs. What night do you think Pomfrey was here?'

'I have a picture,' said Noel hopefully. 'Perhaps if we took it to the front desk …'

Paolo on the front desk rolled his eyes in dismissal. 'Do you know,' he asked, 'how many men come through here? How many of them do you think I remember?' He cast a quick glance at Noel. 'Think I'd know you again mate?'

Noel persisted; two masseurs had regular spots at the sauna.

Rahid, who was on the night Pomfrey died, would be back in two nights. 'Want a booking?' asked Paolo, without much interest as to why Rahid had been chosen.

Michael grinned. 'So,' he said, 'Guess you'll have to come back here.'

cg

While Noel was exploring the many delights of the sauna the official opening of the Conference was drawing to its lengthy conclusion. The ceremony took place in the Millennium Dome, leading to long lines of unhappy delegates as the Jubilee Line struggled to ferry people across London, and hastily upgraded security checks meant yet more lines to enter into the halls. Thankfully, thought Sylvie, the opening ceremony was the only part of the Conference scheduled outside the Westminster and Southbank precincts. She could admire the Dome as a building, with its huge white canopy and the twelve yellow towers scraping the skyline, but as a venue it had given them endless problems.

A children's choir sang an anthem especially composed for the event; Alejandro, over-dressed in a tuxedo with his CBE prominently displayed, had walked minor Royalty to the podium; Spencer, as chief organiser, had delivered housekeeping announcements with the pomp of an eighteenth-century court. Minor Royalty was preceded by a dance troupe from West Africa and an aging Hollywood celebrity, who spoke in mystic terms of love and compassion, words also used by Royalty. A young girl, identified as living proudly with HIV, was ushered on stage to present Royalty with a bouquet of flowers; the princess promptly sneezed which reduced the girl to tears until an assistant ushered her back off stage. A young man representing drug users, nattily dressed in a sky-blue suit, thanked Royalty and paid tribute to Pomfrey, whose face, in a blown-up photograph, hung over the main stage along with the flags of the eighty-six countries present (actually eighty-five, the delegate from one small Caribbean country having been taken violently ill with food poisoning).

Sylvie hovered behind the stage, very aware of Pomfrey's absence. Before she could think further about her future she was distracted by a catering crisis; the kitchen had failed to identify which of the snacks were halal and several delegates, who had wisely found the reception before it officially began, were complaining of AIDS Islamophobia. As she set off for the kitchen to see whether this could be fixed Sylvie noticed Alejandro and Spencer jostling to escort minor Royalty to the reception area.

Alejandro was explaining the search for a vaccine to Royalty, who seemed bemused by the idea of retroviruses and T-cells. 'You see,' he said earnestly, 'Pomfrey and I were collaborating on this promising new lead ...'

'A terrible loss,' said Royalty. Death seemed a safer topic than virology.

Alejandro smiled complacently. 'Of course now I owe it to his memory to continue. We have many distinguished collaborators—Johns Hopkins, the Pasteur Institute, folk in Israel ... Your Highness would appreciate the honour for Britain if we could discover it here.'

Minor Royalty nodded, unconcerned at being addressed with the wrong title, and sipped a glass of champagne. 'I hope you like it ma'am,' said Spencer, anxious not to be left out. 'Veuve cliquot. Not of course that we have it for everyone, we do need to be careful how we spend our resources.'

As soon as she could, minor Royalty departed, wondering whether she could perhaps take on Wimbledon rather than AIDS as her work for the Family. Spencer and Alejandro beamed at each other, their mutual distrust momentarily forgotten. Someone, they thought, needed to succeed Pomfrey as President of the Global AIDS Trust, which would almost certainly lead to a knighthood, if not a peerage. Without any comment they moved apart and hurried off in different directions.

The Advisory Board of the Trust would meet during the Conference and selecting a replacement for Pomfrey was on the agenda. Both men fancied their chances: Alejandro, the leading virologist working on HIV; Spencer, the ultimate organiser who had successfully won the Conference for London and almost doubled attendance. And, he thought smugly, the man who had persuaded British Post to issue a special stamp to commemorate the Conference. On reflection he felt he might have more control were he to remain chief executive and find a more pliable candidate than Pomfrey. Alejandro he distrusted, mainly because he was likely to ask too many awkward questions.

4

A couple of nights later Noel returned to the sauna. It was less busy, but on entering he was accosted by a young man in neat pink shorts and a t-shirt proclaiming, *Test/Stay Safe*, who was carrying a clipboard. 'We're part of a big research project,' he explained, 'from the University. Trying to get an accurate picture of how many men are following safe sex guidelines.'

He handed Noel a flyer; the faces of Pomfrey and Alejandro were displayed, both of them lending their support to the project. 'Did you ever see him here?' asked Noel, pointing at the picture of Pomfrey.

'Not him,' said the man. 'But think I've seen the other one. Alejandro Herrera. He likes to drop in and check on our progress. Don't think he's gay though.'

'But not the other one: Pomfrey Lister?'

The man shook his head and turned to the next person to enter. 'Here,' he said to Noel. 'Take this questionnaire and fill it out for me.'

Noel went back to the entrance and asked about the masseur. Yes, Rahid was on duty; he could have half an hour with him at 8.30. Noel handed over twenty pounds and decided to wait in the pool area.

Rahid was a slim but well-built man dressed in shorts and a tank top, who pointed Noel to the massage table, then carefully covered him with a clean towel. Noel noticed he smelt slightly of lavender oil, and his hair was thick, shiny like black onyx. His fingers ran lightly over Noel's back, then settled into his shoulders and upper back.

'I was wondering,' said Noel tentatively, 'before we begin—' He sat up abruptly and handed Rahid a photograph, a little damp from Noel's towel. 'Any chance you know this man?'

Rahid looked startled, pulled back a little. 'Perhaps,' he said. 'I'm not sure.'

He pushed Noel back onto the table. 'Why do you ask?'

'He's dead,' said Noel. 'Suddenly. And I wondered whether you'd seen him here recently.'

Rahid said nothing, but his grip on Noel's shoulders tightened. 'You knew him well?' he asked.

Noel nodded, as much as he could with his neck still cradled in Rahid's hands.

Rahid thought. 'OK,' he said, pulling back and stretching. 'Sit up for a moment. Tell me why you're here and asking me this question.'

Noel felt suddenly very exposed. 'OK,' he said, 'here's the thing. We knew each other—we were lovers. Sort of. And the night he died I think he might have been here, but he always said he believed in being faithful ...'

Rahid snorted. 'I can hear him saying that.'

'You knew him?'

'Not like that.' Rahid grimaced. 'He was my doctoral supervisor. I knew he was dead—there was a story in the paper.'

'You worked with him?'

Rahid scowled. 'He used me,' he said bitterly. 'He gave me menial jobs in the laboratory while I was writing my thesis, then he pushed me out. After he read the final draft of my thesis he basically dropped me, said it wasn't ready to go to examiners. He even claimed I'd fudged the data.' He grinned ruefully. 'Maybe being a masseur is a better career path than virology.'

He looked hard at Noel. 'So Pomfrey Lister was one of us?' He thought for a moment. 'That might explain why he became so cold with me. Wasn't he married—I think his wife worked for some AIDS charity?'

'Yes. He always claimed he was discreet, even though I met him online.'

Rahid snorted, pushing Noel back onto the table. 'Anyway, I don't think I ever saw him here. Though I'm pretty sure he'd be careful to avoid me.'

He settled into the massage, carefully kneading sore muscles, and Noel felt himself drifting off. 'Just thought,' said Rahid suddenly. 'The night Professor Lister died was leather night at the sauna. Lots of guys wandering around in leather chaps and rubber. That his thing?'

'Oh,' said Noel surprised. 'I'm not sure that I ever really knew him.'

Cg

At home Mary took stock. Even when it is anticipated the death of a partner leaves a gaping void, but Pomfrey's death had happened so abruptly. The first two days moved in a sort of fog, as Mary grappled with the need to hide the realities of his death, to rush through the cremation and ward off curious visitors. After the cremation she went home, took the phone off the hook and drank a fair amount of an expensive bottle of wine that had been saved for a dinner party they would now never host. Mary scorned people who used sleeping pills, but she took one from Pomfrey's stock and slept through. She missed the opening night of the Conference, but on the second day she gathered herself and decided she needed to be seen there.

It seemed another lifetime when they had met, he a promising young virologist, she a volunteer coordinator in a large charity working in Africa on poverty relief. Mary's father had been a civil servant, her mother a teacher; Pomfrey, whose family had inherited wealth, seemed enormously glamorous and worldly. After finishing a nursing diploma, she had studied chemistry at her redbrick University, enough to ask Pomfrey intelligent questions about his work exploring hepatitis viruses, and she was not surprised when Pomfrey rang and asked her to accompany him to a scientific dinner: 'You might be bored,' he warned her, but she was fascinated by the discussion and the after-dinner talk, and soon they started going out together,

There was no special moment, she reflected, no sense of losing herself to the indignities of romantic love, but one long night, when they had both drink a little and the air was warm, Pomfrey invited her back to his then apartment and sex, when it came, was unexpectedly easy if not particularly ecstatic. The best part, she reflected later, was the sense of achievement, of having found someone whom she could imagine spending a life with, someone who shared her ambition to make a difference in the world. Mary was not sexually inexperienced—she had had several boyfriends at university and after—but on the whole, she thought, sex was overrated. Pomfrey was the first man she could imagine settling down with, and if this meant occasional bursts of intimacy that was something she might come in time to enjoy.

When the first AIDS cases were reported—then called Gay Related Immune Deficiency—Pomfrey was in the States, and he quickly became involved in the search, first for the cause and then treatments of the new syndrome. Mary's charity sent her on several field trips to East Africa where she saw some of the early cases in Uganda, comforted young girls now orphaned, some of them expectant mothers in their early teenage years. With her own background and Pomfrey's connections she decided to establish her own AIDS charity, one that would focus on girls at risk from HIV and the sex industry. Mary had grown up in a nominally Protestant family who regarded attendance at church as at best an occasional social duty, but she was increasingly drawn to the nuns and missionaries she met in Africa and heard them preach the safety of abstinence. Under the Bush Administration the Catholic emphasis on chastity had found a new respectability. Government funded posters proclaiming *I'm Proud to be a Virgin* started appearing on the streets of Kampala, and whereas she would once have mocked them, now Mary found herself nodding in agreement.

Sex, she came to believe, was the cause of so much misery, leading people to moments of irrationality that then haunted their lives ever after. She saw young men twisting in agony as the virus decimated their bodies, young girls struggling with the pain of unwanted pregnancies, the anguish of losing babies in still birth and the desperation of trying to hold on to the ones who survived. Luckily Pomfrey had already lost interest in their couplings; over the years love had turned to indifference, maybe at times to a muted hostility, but it suited them both to stay married. She had assumed there might have been other women, but momentary distractions. But over the past few months she had sensed that he had met someone who might threaten their marriage. Now that he was dead she could acknowledge to herself how much she would have hated the dissolution of their marriage, the loss of security and, yes, the material comforts, that Pomfrey provided. Better, perhaps, to be a widow than a discarded spouse.

5

The Conference sprawled across several venues clustered on both sides of the Thames, with the offices and exhibitions in the Princess Diana Centre, a multistorey glass-fronted building with all the charm of a provincial shopping mall. One of the workers on Mary's project was standing nervously in front of a large poster in the exhibition hall, one of a long line of similar exhibits, complex montages of text, photographs, graphs, hypotheses about the latest developments in the HIV/AIDS world. Beside her a large man with a ferocious moustache fronted a poster declaring: *People Living with AIDS are the Future*; opposite several bespectacled nuns stood guard over a far less colourful poster showing a home for wayward girls in Dacca.

Mary greeted her worker and spent the next half hour talking up her project to anyone in earshot. A young woman with pink hair and a nose ring, wearing the t-shirt of a sex worker organisation, passed by and asked surprisingly sympathetic questions; several delegates from East Africa stopped by the poster to thank Mary for the work her organisation was doing. Mary smiled appropriately, not acknowledging that her organisation had badly overspent in the past year and might have to close its Kampala offices.

Spencer sat in his large Conference office on the top floor of the complex and tried taking deep breaths to calm down. The

Conference, so far, was running smoothly, but Spencer was worried. He replayed the events from the night Pomfrey died in his head, looking for cracks in the story they'd agreed upon.

Spencer had grown up in small town America, in a family that belonged to a fundamentalist Protestant church, and he had accepted their strictures about sexuality, even when, as a young student, he found himself lingering too long in men's changing rooms. After sailing through a degree at the state university, an unexpected scholarship had taken him to Yale Law School, home of several recent Presidents. He found law both dull and demanding, faced with fellow students who seemed brighter, and more articulate than any he had come across before. They saw themselves as future Senators or Supreme Court Justices; at best, he thought, he might aspire to a junior partnership in a second tier New York firm. He joined a rowing club and hung around some of the social clubs, his blond good looks and natural charm serving to hide the fact that he was not part of the entitled world to which most of his fellow students belonged.

Arabella St Andrews had been studying art history when she and Spencer met, and theirs was a quick and surprisingly passionate courtship. It was easy for Spencer to abandon his plans for a law career and move to England with Arabella, tempted by promises of working for her father's enterprises, which straddled several continents and generated generous profits. Spencer soon established himself as an efficient and imaginative manager, and marriage followed effortlessly. Arabella's family enveloped Spencer, who started to model himself on the older men in the exclusive London clubs where he was now a frequent guest. Predictably he became a first-class snob, echoing attitudes no longer fashionable; when his own mother visited he was embarrassed by her clothes and her religious precepts, which now seemed very distant from his own life.

When AIDS first emerged in the early 1980s Spencer regarded it as yet another media beat up, but a cousin of Arabella was an early patient, and Spencer found himself caught between his own squeamishness and his wife's ease in London gay society. Through her cousin Arabella had become close to a group of artists and theatre performers, most of them gay, and she was one of the first donors to early AIDS charities. After an evening where he almost met Elton John and Ian McKellen, Spencer decided that maybe he should take an interest in the disease.

He had recently taken up a role as chief operating officer of one of her father's companies, when Sir Malcolm St Andrews recommended he apply for the chief executive position at the Global AIDS Trust. The Trust was essentially a group of well-connected medicos and philanthropists, and Spencer was reassured by its sheer respectability and the list of patrons, several of whom he already knew through Arabella. If, as some suspected, he was appointed over several better qualified candidates it was in part because he was demonstrably not a gay man.

He became a regular guest at fund-raising events for various AIDS organisations, at one of which he met Joe. It was a large event in one of the fashionable Mayfair hotels; Arabella was away that evening and Spencer was seated beside a large, marine-cropped man who introduced himself as Joe Tripaldi, electrician, noting ruefully that he was usually the only one at this sort of event. But when Spencer, unsure how to proceed, began a desultory conversation he was surprised to discover how well-informed Joe was about the latest medical reports and the promising advances in HIV treatments. Over dinner Joe mentioned he had an electrician and plumber working for him, as part of his Pink Tradesman services. A week later Joe turned up at Spencer's Knightsbridge house—set in a discreet row of mew houses, in an apparent cul-de-sac—with a young tradie in tow, and the two of them sipped cold cider on the terrace while the trainee electrician went to work.

Spencer was quietly congratulating himself on his tolerance in employing a gay tradesman, when Joe made a chance remark about his girlfriend.

'But,' said Spencer cautiously, 'aren't you ...?'

'Mate,' said Joe, 'it's all about the marketing. I don't need to screw with my clients. I was at the dinner to be seen by potential customers.'

Joe was a skilled electrician who had first discovered the possibilities of a gay market by branding himself as the pink electrician, even though he was not himself homosexual. Through one of his customers he invested in a bed and breakfast in Brighton and spent several weekends checking out the venues in that city, looking for other opportunities. He enjoyed hanging around gay bars, which lacked the simmering aggression of the pubs he would go to with his football mates, sizing up possible investments. After the success of the Brighton house he became a partner in a small gay bar in Hastings, but his dream was to buy an existing run-down sauna in London and make it a fashionable gay venue, for which he needed considerable capital.

'Yes,' said Spencer, 'a couple of my colleagues have told me about saunas—bathhouses, they call them in the States. They thought they were spreading the virus, and cities like San Francisco and New York closed them down. Silly really, they are good places for messaging and contact tracing. We need saunas that will cooperate.'

'I even went to a couple of saunas,' said Joe. 'Those guys—it's a lot easier for them than it is for us hetero blokes. Walk in, strip down, and suddenly you're in poofter heaven.' He sipped his drink reflectively. 'But a city like London just doesn't have the scale of saunas you find in Paris, Amsterdam. There's a goldmine there if you do it right.'

He looked reflectively at Spencer. 'Don't suppose you'd be interested in investing? It's a sure thing.'

Spencer smiled uneasily. 'I don't think I could ...'

'I have a few investors already lined up: no-one except me gets to hold more than 20% and I keep control. Of course it's all kept very confidential, bank accounts in Guernsey, none of the partners' names made public. And,' he added, 'our sauna would be a perfect place for your research surveys.'

That conversation with Joe lingered in his mind over the next weeks. With access to the accounts of the Trust, Spencer had made some risky choices, one of which paid off; he was too embarrassed to declare the amount to his accountant or to explain to Pomfrey how he had risked the money. Unexpectedly he found himself with a considerable sum that had to be hidden and Joe, he thought, might be the person to help. Of course, he reassured himself, this was strictly a financial proposition, but the idea of a sauna, full of naked men in search of sex, both tantalised and repelled him.

A properly run sauna, Spencer reassured himself, would be an asset in responding to the epidemic and a money-earner for the Trust. And if his involvement were kept secret … He decided to at least follow up with another meeting, and after some hesitation agreed that the Trust would become a silent investor in the Spartacus Sauna, London's *biggest, gayest, raunchiest meeting place for men who like men.* Every time Spencer read those words he grimaced, but Joe insisted that the returns promised to be excellent.

A knock on the door and Spencer was jolted back into the present. Sylvie had an urgent problem with the next plenary session. A former British cabinet minister had arrived to chair a panel of First Ladies speaking on *Mobilising the People to Fight HIV* and refused to participate when she realised the entire panel consisted of wives and daughters of political leaders, at least two of whom were known to have killed their opponents.

'If only Pomfrey were here,' sighed Spencer. 'He could have handled it.'

'Spencer,' said Sylvie, 'Do you think his death was surprising? Odd, even?'

'Odd?' Spencer scratched his nose vigorously. 'Odd in what way?'

'I never thought he had heart problems,' said Sylvie.

Spencer nodded. 'He was a very private person, of course. He wouldn't have admitted any weaknesses to us.'

'No,' said Sylvie sadly, 'I suppose not. But—it all felt so rushed. The death. The very fast cremation.'

'Mary insisted. A very strong woman—not,' he added, 'that I

know her that well.' Better, he thought, if Sylvie assumed they were merely acquaintances.

They entered the plenary hall, lined with memorial quilts of those who had died from AIDS, with a hastily added image of Pomfrey hung above the stage, where four first ladies were importantly arranging themselves—the wife of one Central Asian despot, Sylvie explained in a whisper, had gone shopping and had not been seen for two days. The replacement chair was an elegant Latin American parliamentarian, who had actually been elected, and who insisted on a Spanish interpreter, despite having perfectly acceptable English. 'This is an international Conference after all,' she stressed, and there was a delay while Alejandro was called in to fill the role.

'Not really appropriate,' he grumbled, though not unhappy to be back on the stage, displaying his fluency in both languages. Alejandro was proud of being both an English gentleman and a Colombian of Spanish origin and was equally snobbish in both guises. One of his forebears might have served under Bolivar during the nineteenth century wars of independence, and Alejandro was constantly annoyed by the ignorance of his British peers when he mentioned the fact. At school they called him the young Bolivar, and it was not meant kindly.

The problem with translating, he thought, was that it meant listening carefully to every speaker, all of whom repeated the stock phrases that now accompanied the language of the epidemic, only one of them, it seemed, able to draw on any experience of having known someone with HIV. One of the speakers managed to sound authoritative for eight minutes without once mentioning the actual epidemic.

Following the panel Alejandro and Spencer walked back to the Conference offices together, conscious that something had changed between them. Until two nights ago they had been colleagues through the Trust, certainly not friends; now they shared an uneasy feeling of having collaborated in ways that could be deeply embarrassing were it to be too widely known.

Spencer, who in his new-found Englishness still thought of Alejandro as a foreigner, was very aware that Alejandro might have been surprised that he was at Pomfrey's house the evening of his death. Mary had presumably explained his and Joe's presence without mentioning the sauna, though how he wasn't sure. Thinking back he realised Alejandro had been surprisingly quick to arrive at the house, and very vague as to where he'd been that evening, though his clothes looked as if they had been thrown on rather hurriedly. How little we know about the people we work with, thought Spencer, aware that he had never seen Alejandro with anyone of either sex who might be his partner.

Pomfrey had been closer to each of them; Alejandro as a fellow virologist, Spencer as the chief organiser of the Conference of which Pomfrey had been chair. Alejandro had been given the meaningless title of Deputy, which now put him in a position to replace Pomfrey. The two of them had been collaborating on what seemed a promising lead for an HIV vaccine, but there were signs of tension between them; what these were, thought Spencer, might be worth investigating. He had an uneasy sense that were Alejandro to become the chair of the Trust his own position might be in jeopardy. All the more reason to find an alternative successor as chair.

6

Sylvie had spent the first two nights of the Conference at a nearby hotel so as to be ready for any last-minute crises. On the third day she decided to return home and have the evening to herself. An instant dinner in front of television—*Midsomer Murders* perhaps—seemed more attractive than yet another anxious dinner with self-important dignitaries.

She surveyed the depressingly empty freezer and decided on frozen lasagne. She was just taking it out of the microwave when the phone rang.

'Noel?' she answered.

'Can we talk?' he asked, conscious of repeating the cliché. 'I feel there's something wrong about Pomfrey's death.'

Sylvie sighed. 'Noel,' she said, 'am I really the person to talk to about this?'

'But you're the only person who knew us both and knew what we meant to each other.'

Sylvie thought. 'OK,' she said reluctantly, 'maybe you'd better come over.' She looked at the cooling lasagne and tipped it into the rubbish bin, taking out a bottle of wine and a chunk of onion-flavoured cheddar.

Thirty minutes later a slightly out of breath Noel showed up at her flat. It was on a small cul-de-sac off the main road, at the rear of a four-storey building which seemed dwarfed by the towering council flats around it. Finding a decent apartment that close to the centre had thrilled Sylvie, despite the taboos that surrounded an area of run-down housing estates.

'Even Karl Marx wrote about Kennington' she remarked, as she poured out wine for them. 'There's a line in *Das Kapital* where he says that Kennington was very seriously over-populated in 1859, when diphtheria appeared.'

'I haven't read Marx,' said Noel, aware as usual of his political naivete.

'Me neither. I found that quote online.'

It was the first time Noel had been there, and his first impression was of a well-kept impersonality and neat, if unremarkable, furnishings, bought from one of the new Ikea stores. The lounge was small, with two comfortable chairs beside a low coffee table, strewn with Conference papers and the latest editions of *New Stateman* and *Private Eye*.

Wine poured, and the necessary introductory remarks—the cremation; the Conference; Noel's work in the bookshop—dispensed with, Noel bent forward.

'I think Pomfrey was out the night he died,' he said. 'I think he might have been at a sauna before he collapsed.'

'A gay sauna?' Sylvie pondered. 'Would he take the risk?—and on the eve of the Conference? Mary was very clear that he died at home.'

'I need to know, Sylvie. I just don't know how to find out. The only person who might be able to help is a masseur there, who knew Pomfrey—maybe you knew him? a student of Pomfrey's called Rahid? Good-looking guy, little shorter than me, very thick black hair?'

'Yes,' said Sylvie, 'I vaguely remember. Pomfrey thought he'd cheated on a lab test, but he denied it. Think there was a row, and the student disappeared.'

'I think he knows something. Can you help me find him— somewhere outside the sauna?'

Sylvie opened her newly acquired home Macintosh and searched for a file. 'Rahid,' she said, 'there are two people with that name here.' She pointed to a master list of volunteers working at the Conference. 'Could he be one of these?'

'I guess,' said Noel, 'I could check them out. Do you know when they'll be at the Conference?'

Sylvie tapped a couple of keys but could find little more information. 'The best thing,' she said, 'is to float around and hope you catch sight of the one you're after. But what do you think you'll find out?'

'I don't really know. Don't you feel there's something about Pomfrey's death that's ... a little strange?'

'Yes,' she said, thinking aloud. 'It all seemed too fast: the sudden death, the cremation with hardly anyone there. As if Mary knew something was wrong.'

She looked at Noel. 'Did she ... know about you and Pomfrey?'

Noel thought. 'I don't think so. I know Pomfrey was very careful, he knew Mary had strong religious beliefs. She might have guessed that he liked men, but it wasn't something they would ever have talked about.'

'And you never met?'

'God no. Pomfrey was very careful, we only saw each other when he was certain she was well out of the way. But maybe you could ask Mary more about the night he died?'

Sylvie shook her head. 'I wouldn't feel comfortable doing that. But perhaps I could talk to Alejandro. I know Mary called him in that night rather than their own doctor.'

Sylvie pondered how best to approach Alejandro. Normally he would be at either his laboratory or the hospital, but with Pomfrey gone he had worked himself into a frenzy of Conference activity, rushing from session to session, grabbing colleagues in the corridors, hosting small dinners with the international members of the Global AIDS Trust. His one relaxation, she knew, was to play tennis, and Sylvie had a vague memory that one of her friends on the vaccine research project was a member of his tennis club.

'The Conference ends this weekend. After that I can hunt her up. And meanwhile—' She rummaged around the papers on the table. 'Here's a pass for the Conference centre. Go look for your elusive masseur.'

She picked up her phone. 'Now,' she sighed, 'I have to go sort out some accommodation hassles. One of the Canadians claims there's no air conditioning in her hotel and she is suffocating.'

_____ ∞ _____

Caitlin Graham was uneasy. She had been thrilled, only six months after finishing her doctorate, to be employed in the research laboratory which was led by Pomfrey and Alejandro, and she was excited by the work. Like everyone else on the project she had seen young men die of excruciating illnesses, and even now, with effective therapies available, a vaccine for HIV could save millions of lives. As a graduate student she had been fascinated by retroviruses, and the problems of developing ways to eradicate them; now she was working with two of the top scientists in the field.

She was used to trials on mice but she was more squeamish when it came to experimental therapies on rhesus monkeys. 'Think of the payoff,' Pomfrey had told her. 'The young girls in Zambia and Namibia and the Philippines who don't get access to therapies and are getting infected by older men.' A small consignment of rhesus macaques had arrived several months earlier, and she avoided the section of the laboratories where they were housed. She was relieved that her duties were confined to test tubes and computers.

But she had overheard at least one heated discussion between Pomfrey and Alejandro about the progress of the rhesus trials, and she saw Pomfrey leave the animal house shaking his head, clearly disturbed by what had happened. In the rigid hierarchies of medical research, she hadn't dared ask if there was a problem.

Her work gave her little direct contact with Alejandro, and she had been startled, and a little embarrassed, when she joined a suburban tennis club and discovered he was a regular player. He nodded at her, clearly indicating that any contact they had in the laboratories was not to be mentioned at the tennis club. Curiosity piqued, she decided to find out more about him.

Alejandro was a young consultant when the first AIDS cases showed up at St Mary's Hospital, and he quickly attached himself to one of the major research teams that was trying to unravel the mysteries of the new virus. As the epidemic spread he found himself sitting on government advisory panels and talking on late night chat shows, enjoying the role of AIDS expert as his contact with patients diminished. His partnership with Pomfrey seemed a natural progression, and the lure of discovering a vaccine for HIV increasingly preoccupied him. As a retrovirus it was remarkably resistant to eradication: the virus is able to integrate into the host cell genome, but does not proceed to active replication, and sits there waiting to re-emerge.

She knew that Alejandro had been born in Colombia, and she assumed he had been brought onto the council of the Global AIDS Trust because he could satisfy both the British need to dominate and the Latin American claims for representation. About his private life she knew nothing: a search of *Who's Who* revealed a wife (Isabella) and one son (Carlos), but nothing more. She knew he was passionate about the work of the laboratories; whether this was because of ambition or some more personal reason she had no idea. But a few weeks ago, when a few of them were chatting on the sidelines, waiting to go onto the tennis courts, he'd made a comment about starting human trials as soon as possible, and how one could be too cautious when lives were at stake.

പ

Entering the main halls of the Conference left Noel bewildered. He stood in the entrance reading the signs: *Exhibition Hall; Plenary Sessions; Break Out Rooms; First Aid; Prayer Room; People Living With HIV Lounge* ... in all this activity where might he come across Rahid?

Maybe, he thought, the cafeteria; he could get coffee and sit there for a while in the hope that Rahid might wander in. But after three quarters of an hour, during which he drank two weak cappuccinos and ate a deeply pink donut, there was no sign of Rahid. He decided to walk round the Centre, maybe get a feel for the Conference by visiting some of the exhibitors stands. The main exhibition area was a large high-ceilinged space on the ground floor of the Centre, where big pharmaceutical companies and medical suppliers jostled for attention, well-groomed spruikers handing out free coffees, ice-creams, tote bags, pens ... Noel had grown up in the shadow of AIDS, had learnt to use condoms as part of his initiation into gay life, but now he realised how little he knew about the virus. With Pomfrey dead he felt he owed it to him to learn something about his work.

Suddenly energised he went into one of the plenary halls, where a speaker was laboriously working his way through a large set of overheads, but what, thought Noel desperately, are protease inhibitors? reverse transcriptase? lipodystrophy? Maybe another presentation would be easier; in an adjoining hall a man with a shock of long dark hair and a deeply furrowed face was talking about the efficacy of needle exchanges. Noel, who felt faint when blood was taken, had never understood the lure of shooting up, but he was glad that those who did could be protected from infection.

He had come into the room towards the end of the session and now a few people leapt to the mike to ask questions, most of which seemed to be statements that suggested the speakers had missed vital points. When one woman began her question by saying she needed to talk about her own experience, and how she had freed herself from heroin through meditation and yoga, Noel decided to leave.

Outside the room he saw a small group of young women wearing the distinctive red and white t-shirts of Conference volunteers. 'Excuse me,' he said, 'do any of you know a guy called Rahid, he's a volunteer here?'

'I think so,' said one. 'He's in charge of the cultural program.'

'So where would I find him?'

'Their offices are across the river,' she said. 'That's where they've put the culture and the community offices.'

The Conference had taken over several buildings between the Millennium Wheel and the National Theatre, and here the atmosphere was more festive, no earnest sessions or poster exhibits, but rather a sense of expectation, a swirl of noise and colour as delegates assembled for the traditional Conference march and protest. What they were protesting was not clear to most, but the march had been programmed for some months and protest they would. Noel ducked through a rowdy group of women carrying the red umbrellas of the sex worker movement and went inside in search of the cultural offices.

Rahid was sitting at a small desk, scrolling down through his computer screen. If he was surprised to see Noel he hid it well.

'So,' he said, swivelling round to look straight at Noel, 'you've decided to stalk me?'

He really was a very good-looking man thought Noel, gulping. 'No,' he said. 'That is—I want your help.'

'I've already told you. I have no idea if Prof. Lister was at the sauna that night. I've never seen him there.'

'There must be records?'

'People sign in, but no one checks their ID. You'd be surprised how many times Mickey Mouse visits. Or Prince Edward.'

Noel sighed. 'I'm not even sure why it matters,' he said. 'But I'd really like to know whether that's where he spent his last night—before he died. I think something might have happened to him, something that explains the heart attack.' He looked at Rahid. 'You must know other punters who were there that night?'

'A couple. But doubt they'd take well to you asking them a lot of questions.' Rahid stood up. 'Look,' he said, 'you seem like a nice guy, not sure what you were doing getting mixed up with Pomfrey Lister. I'll ask around for you. Okay?'

'It's strange,' said Noel, 'that I care so much. But if he was there just before he died I feel I need to know. I'd hate to think that he was with another man.'

'Yeah,' said Rahid. 'Jealousy. Totally irrational and yet we can't wish it away. Maybe that's how you figure out how much you cared for him.'

Rahid knew that Pomfrey had been at the sauna that night, but he felt it better that Noel found that out from someone else. Or perhaps remained ignorant. He stood up. 'You joining the march mate?'

A vague distrust of politics meant Noel had always avoided demonstrations; when he remembered to vote he was a Labour supporter, mainly because his mother had been a trade unionist. At University, where he had studied English and Psychology until he dropped out and found work in the bookshop, he had been intimidated by the more radical students, and it was only in his third year that he'd found the courage to attend meetings of the GLBT student group. For several years now he'd watched the parade at London Pride, not feeling free to join, though he occasionally went to events at the *Gay's the Word* Bookshop, where he had a nodding acquaintance with the owners. But tempting as it was to spend more time with Rahid he muttered something about having to go back to the shop and left before the Conference protest rallied.

On the tube back to his bookshop he thought through what he knew. If Pomfrey was at the sauna that night was it perhaps to meet someone? Or was he there on a whim? If Rahid would not help, other people would have been working at the sauna that night. He had a vague memory of a young guy who was cleaning the floors the night he was there, and presumably there would be other staff. Cheered by the prospect of action he decided to go back to the sauna that evening.

It was still light when he entered and was let in by the same bored teller who showed no sign of remembering him. The locker room was empty; upstairs a couple of men prowled the corridors without any sign of contact.

Noel went back to the pool, where a young guy, dressed only in denim shorts, was cleaning the jacuzzi.

'Hello,' said Noel tentatively.

The boy swivelled around, seemingly alarmed. He was disconcertingly young, thought Noel, with a slightly twisted mouth and thick curly hair, which drooped low across his forehead.

'Sorry,' said Noel. 'But I was wondering—were you here a few nights ago—last Wednesday?'

The boy thought. 'Probably not, boss. What's up?'

'I'm trying to find out if someone was here. He's dead now.'

'Oh.' The boy scratched absently at his thigh. 'Well I think Winston might have been on that night. He usually does the cleaning on my nights off.'

'So he'll be here tomorrow then?'

'It's funny, that,' said the boy reflectively. 'He's gone. Joe—the manager, like, said he was paid out last week. Figured he wanted to leave.'

'Do you know where he lives?'

'Nah, not as if we were friends, like. But I remember him talking about hanging out at a couple of pubs near the theatres—Shaftesbury Avenue, I guess?'

'What's he look like?'

The boy grinned. 'Well, lots whiter than me, boss. Taller, sort of skinny. With a mohawk—or he had, last time I saw him.'

Noel sighed. Trawling through the bars of Soho looking for a skinny guy with a mohawk seemed a long shot.

The boy lowered his voice. 'I think,' he said conspiratorially, 'he might have been on the game. Maybe he'd go with older blokes for money when he was skint.'

Later that evening, as he wandered disconsolately around the sauna, Noel would brood on those words. Was it possible that Pomfrey had paid this guy—Winston—for sex? Is that why he was at the sauna that evening—if indeed he had been. Noel decided he needed to track down Winston.

He was about to leave when he realised a plumpish older man, with a slightly wispy beard, was staring meaningfully at him. Not my type thought Noel, but maybe he might know where to find

Winston. A tentative smile and the man, Godfrey his name, came closer, so that their bare thighs touched.

'Hello,' said Godfrey, his voice surprisingly deep. 'You want to find a room?'

No, thought Noel, but he nodded, and Godfrey was steering him back to the corridor lined with small cubicles, furnished only with low beds and condom dispensers. They entered; Godfrey reached up to kiss him.

'No,' said Noel, clutching at his towel which was draped low on his hips. 'That is—not so fast—I'm really only here to find someone.'

'Someone?' Godfrey ran his arm across Noel's shoulder. 'I'm someone.'

'No,' said Noel, turning away. 'A guy called Winston. Used to work here.'

'Winston?' Godfrey chuckled. 'Aren't you a bit young for him mate?'

'You know him?'

'Yes.' Godfrey chuckled again. 'But what do you want with him?'

'Where would I find him?'

'Good question, mate.' Godfrey moved away and looked hard at Noel. 'You don't want to screw do you?'

'Not really,' said Noel. 'But I do want to find Winston—it's not sex or anything, just need to ask him a question.'

'OK'. Godfrey thought for a moment. 'You might try one of the pubs on Wardour Street. You might find someone there more to your liking.' He grabbed at Noel's arm. 'Unless you want to go at it now?'

Noel hesitated; the man's very persistence could be a turn on. But no, he said, and slipped out of the cubicle. At the end of the corridor stood a short dark-haired man with a lightly muscled body, but when Noel smiled at him he turned abruptly and walked away. Discouraged Noel decided to go home.

7

Meanwhile Spencer and Alejandro were preparing for a small but crucial dinner. The seven international governors of the Trust had been invited to a gentlemen's club off Park Lane and a distinguished author would be guest of honour. The governors had been carefully chosen to be both eminent and unlikely to interfere, most of them women and men with long and distinguished careers which now found them on many advisory boards and business class flights. They had all known Pomfrey, and appropriate regrets were muttered as Mary entered the room where pre-drink cocktails were being served.

'I need to talk to you,' she whispered to Spencer, as yet another of the governors, a retired judge from south Asia, took her hand and expressed his deepest sympathies.

'So brave, dear lady,' he said, 'to attend this dinner.' He lowered his voice. 'Some of us wonder whether you might, in time, consider the possibility of joining us on the advisory board. Only once you feel up to a new commitment, of course, dear lady.'

He took her arm and steered her into the private dining room, a large rectangular room with thick carpets and walls lined with portraits of former Club Presidents—all male, she noted, and all white, uncomfortable in bushy moustaches and wing-collars.

Women were admitted as guests, and made up the majority of the staff, but any suggestion that they be given membership had been firmly rejected. They were seated at a long table, elegantly set with plates that bore the insignia of the Club's founder, the third Earl of Clifton, who had built a fortune in Malay tea and rubber and retired to become a dependable Tory vote in the Lords, provided he could stay awake and sober. Young attendants, dressed in the uncomfortable livery of the club, hovered behind them to pour wine, one arm bent correctly behind their backs. When one of the male guests started to remove his jacket a waiter tapped him discretely on the shoulder and reminded him that was not done.

The menu was predictable, although the inclusion of vegetarian ravioli was clearly a sop to the occasional guest who might prefer to avoid the roast lamb or pheasant en croute. Mary was seated between Alejandro and Elvira Blomvquist, a distinguished epidemiologist from Norway, whom she had met on a field trip to Rwanda. They quickly slipped into reminiscing: the generosity of people who had so little, the long meetings with government officials in rooms that were always too hot, despite the overhead fans, the cultural evening, which had dragged on long into the night.

'When all we wanted was to go back to the hotel and sleep!' said Elvira. 'And that long ride back to the hotel, with the one mosquito that kept buzzing around the bus, terrifying half a dozen doctors with the thought of dengue.' She put her hand on Mary's arm. 'So,' she said, 'how are you coping?'

'Please,' said Mary, 'don't ask me that. It's just—I get so tired of people caring. I know everyone means well, but it just makes it worse. Some things just can't be undone.' She turned towards Alejandro, who was pondering the dessert choice between sorbet framboise and baked toffee pudding.

'I wanted to thank you,' she said carefully, 'for coming over the other night. It just seemed better to call in someone who knew us.'

Alejandro nodded, still preoccupied with the menu: profiteroles also looked tempting.

'And you had a long way to come?' said Mary. 'You live outside London I think.'

'Yes. Yes, but I was in town that night, visiting—checking up on one of our projects.'

They were interrupted by Spencer's introduction of the guest speaker, who had been invited because she had written an essay which was widely believed to be about AIDS, although she never used the term. A tall woman, with a mane of luxuriant white hair, she was a commanding presence, with the self-confidence of someone who knows herself to be the smartest person in the room. She had chosen to speak on Culture and Health, about the crucial role of performers, dancers, *writers* in an age dominated by the empirical and the pragmatic. 'If we do not feed the spirit,' she declaimed, 'what point is there in feeding the body?' At least one of her listeners, an eminent surgeon from Cape Town, snorted, wondering how many starved bodies the writer had actually encountered.

'This is a waste of time,' hissed the surgeon to the person next to her, but Spencer had chosen a guest speaker deliberately to prevent too much discussion of the future of the Trust.

The dinner over—Alejandro having settled for the pudding— they moved into a smaller but equally richly furnished drawing room for coffee and liqueurs. Mary took Spencer's arm and led him onto the terrace.

'I'm worried,' she said. 'About our mission.'

'*God Loves Us All?*' said Spencer, 'I thought you were doing wonderful work.'

'Not everyone thinks so.' Mary looked over the small garden that backed onto a private car park, once the stables of a ducal estate. 'There seems to be some concern about how I run things.'

'But you're the heart of the organisation. Without you what is there?'

'That's it.' Mary was not someone who liked admitting weakness. 'Some of the workers feel I am too controlling. The ones on the ground claim they should decide what projects to fund. The ones here complain they're not paid enough.' She snorted. 'They want to set up a collective to make decisions.'

'But,' said Spencer, 'would that jeopardise our key messages? I always felt the emphasis on family and keeping out western ideas of sexual licence was our strong point.'

'They think targeting homosexuals is too dangerous.'

'Well, perhaps,' said Spencer judiciously. 'Not my views of course. But we are in step with the governments of East Africa after all.'

Mary nodded. 'Yes, the President's wife, Janet, was very gracious.'

She recalled her last trip to Entebbe, the steps leading up to the white portico where First Lady Janet Museveni had greeted a delegation of foreign aid workers. They had milled around in the garden, shaded by heavy palm trees, were then ushered onto uncomfortable white rattan chairs to hear the President's wife address them.

'She is very big on abstinence,' agreed Mary. 'And if we are against homosexuality it is to prevent unrestrained spread of HIV across the continent.'

'How much real discontent is there?' asked Spencer. 'Enough to challenge you?'

Mary looked uncomfortable, not sure how far she could trust Spencer. She had uneasy memories of a discussion with the head of the London office staff who had told her bluntly that unless they found new donors the organisation would need to close several of its programs, and that apart from their pay the staff were increasingly unhappy with what they saw as a one-woman organisation. 'If we're to survive,' her manager had said, 'we need a new structure. Maybe it's time for you to take more of a back seat, let the people who do the work steer the projects.'

'So unfair,' said Mary, losing her composure for a moment. '*God Loves Us All* only exists because of my vision.'

'About that,' said Spencer tentatively, 'how would you feel about coming into partnership with the Global AIDS Trust? You and I working together could be very powerful. Ours is a righteous cause, after all.'

And, he thought, they both shared information he'd prefer was not more widely known. Were Alejandro to take over he might ask too many embarrassing questions which perhaps Mary could fend off. Spencer had spent much of the evening sounding out Trust members about the next chair, reassuring them that while Alejandro was, of course, the logical successor he would have an added load in the laboratories now that he alone could head the search for an HIV vaccine, that maybe the best way to honour Pomfrey was to invite his wife—herself a distinguished figure in the AIDS world—to replace him.

After the dinner Mary went home, stopping for unnecessary groceries at the Muswell Hill shops. She felt reluctant to enter the house, empty in a way it had not been even when Pomfrey was travelling. Pomfrey had increasingly slept in a single bed in the second bedroom; now she took over that room for herself, not wanting to disturb memories of their marriage. In time, if she stayed in the house, she would get rid of the double bed, refashion the room to remove too many traces of Pomfrey.

છ

The last day of the Conference saw both Spencer and Alejandro quietly canvassing the Trust board members. By the end of six days the delegates were weary, and the closing session saw numbers steadily decline, as speeches seemed to lengthen in proportion to the boredom of their listeners. An elegantly dressed American woman, speaking on behalf of sex workers, spent most of her allotted time complaining that sex workers were not given a place on the program. A senior cabinet minister arrived, pledged renewed government commitment— 'Britain,' he proclaimed, 'wants to hear from those of you leading a global mobilisation against this pandemic'—and rushed back to his department. Spencer had arranged a hastily assembled montage of photos of Pomfrey, which were played in the background as the most venerable member of the Trust Advisory Board read out a tribute.

Spencer and Alejandro waited tensely to find out whether any decision had been made about Pomfrey's replacement, but the other members of the Board had agreed to leave it unresolved for now.

Speeches over, the Conference concluded with a children's choir, and a moment of silence for all those who had died from AIDS.

Spencer took the opportunity to beckon Mary into a quiet corner.

'I'm worried,' he said. 'I thought they had agreed to our plan, now this sudden delay.'

'Does the chair of the Trust have to be British?'

'I don't think there's any provision in the rules for choosing the chair,' said Spencer. 'We never thought about it as long as Pomfrey was there. But maybe the trustees have someone else in mind.' He looked anxious. 'None of them seem to want to talk to me about it.'

Indeed the seven foreign trustees seemed to have largely withdrawn from contact with both him and Alejandro, and Spencer had an alarming glimpse of them huddled together on the side of the main Conference Hall, ignoring the Latvian dance troupe now on stage. More disturbingly, Elvira Blomvquist had said she was staying on in London after the Conference and she would come by the office, 'to familiarise herself with the details'.

The Trustees, had decided, she told him, to defer choosing a replacement for Pomfrey until they knew whether the Conference had been a financial success.

ଔ

Following the ceremony Sylvie went home, surprised at how much she was looking forward to domestic chores. After dealing with delegate's requests for last minute changes to flights or helping to replace lost Blackberries, washing the sheets seemed surprisingly attractive. She threw off her shoes and reached for a glass of wine, making a mental note that she needed to stock up on groceries. As if on cue the phone rang: Noel.

'Please Sylvie,' he said, 'I need someone to come with me.'

Sylvie sighed. The prospect of an evening searching the gay pubs of Soho was hardly how she wanted to spend her first free time after the Conference.

'It could be fun,' said Noel. 'A couple of drinks on a warm evening—and we won't stay long in any of the bars.'

Noel was familiar with a few gay pubs, particularly the Black Cap, which was his local hangout, and had once been taken to the *City of Quebec* in Marylebone, but he knew the area around Shaftesbury Avenue for its secondhand books rather than its gay venues. He often visited the dealers who had storefronts on and around Cecil Court, and he'd sometimes stopped for a late afternoon drink in one of the nearby pubs, but he was more likely to go to one of the little cafés further up into Soho. Noel had discovered his sexuality during the dark days of the AIDS epidemic, before effective therapies against infection had been invented, and it was only in his thirties that he'd discovered the joys of outdoor cruising, then of online hook ups. He had spent little time in pubs and bars, and he was oddly timid in overtly gay environments.

'Skinny, with a mohawk,' he repeated to her. 'Rather out of fashion isn't it?'

They were sipping beer in the corner of a large pub that fronted out onto a cramped intersection. The large lounge area surrounded a long semicircular bar, where appropriately buff barmen poured, mixed, charged credit cards and chatted with regular customers. The room was framed by heavy wooden beams, a contrast to the much newer glass windows opening onto the street; in one corner stood a couple of old armchairs, remnants of an earlier moment in the pub's history, where two large men, balding but with untamed facial hair, defied anyone to unseat them. It was early evening, and a steady stream of drinkers swirled in and out, office workers, tradesmen coming off shifts, the occasional group of young women out for the night, high heels and shiny purses.

'It doesn't look very gay to me,' said Sylvie, looking across the lounge.

But there was at least one group of younger men in the pub, four or five, dressed in cargo pants and t-shirts, caps pulled backwards, and Noel gestured to them.

'Should I ask—?' he said, unwilling to broach the group.

'Let's try somewhere else,' suggested Sylvie.

The sun was still low in the sky, and the streets were increasingly full, the pubs marked by crowds of men, often in tank tops and shorts, drinking on the narrow footpaths. Most of the men had short, aggressively short hair, which would make a mohawk stand out, but they saw no-one who fitted the description Noel had been given.

'There must be an easier way to find this guy,' said Sylvie, after her second shandy. She was feeling slightly light-headed, her feet hurt, and she wanted to go home. Noel could continue to trawl the bars and streets of Soho, but without her.

'OK,' he said doubtfully, 'I'll walk you to the tube.'

Noel left her near Cambridge Circus and retraced their steps back into Soho. The evening was becoming hazy, the sun beginning to dip beneath the skyline, casting long shadows on the ground. Noel felt torn, unwilling to give up the search for Winston, tantalised by the idea of plunging back into the streets and finding sex, uncomplicated physical relief that might distract him from the growing need to discover whether Pomfrey really had been at the sauna that night.

Walking back along Frith Street Noel passed a men's hairdresser, with images of men's hairdos carefully posted alongside the shop entrance. He was struck by one of the photographs, a thin white guy, with a slightly blotchy skin and a long, slightly hooked nose, wearing tight distressed jeans and purple sneakers, topped by a carefully shaped faux mohawk. Unlikely that this was Winston, yes, but it suggested a new possibility of finding him. Noel figured there were only a handful of hairdressers in London where a gay man needing a mohawk would go, but without a picture of

Winston that was no more likely to provide a lead than the pubs of Soho.

C８

The following morning Sylvie was due to meet with Mary. She approached the house with some trepidation, wondering about her relationship with Mary and whether it would survive Pomfrey's death. As usual she found Mary seated in the living room, dressed in a subdued skirt and blouse which accentuated her large but rather shapely figure. Sylvie thought she looked older, grief having left dark circles around her eyes and a slight drooping of the neck.

Coffee was poured, the necessary preliminaries dispatched with.

'You know,' said Mary, 'how fond Pomfrey was of you—we both are. I hope you can keep working closely with the Trust.'

She handed Sylvie a piece of seed cake, bent forward.

'Tell me, my dear,' she said, 'did Pomfrey ever express any concerns about the finances of the Trust?'

Sylvie paused. 'No,' she said thoughtfully. 'Not directly. But I did wonder ...'

'Yes?' Mary leant forward.

'Nothing really,' said Sylvie. 'Just a couple of messages ... I'm sure everything was okay. He left all of that to Spencer.'

'Yes,' said Mary thoughtfully. 'Well, I'm sure it's all in capable hands. Nothing to concern you.' She leant forward. 'I think the Trust is in danger of losing sight of what is most important. If there's not a strong moral compass guiding its work it can't succeed in its mission. Now that Pomfrey has died I owe it to him to help steer the Trust in the right direction.'

She stopped talking for a moment, looking hard at Sylvie. 'You were very fond of Pomfrey I think?'

'Yes,' said Sylvie, 'I was. He gave me opportunities I would never have imagined.'

'And you were close?' Mary hesitated, not sure what she wanted to ask.

'Not really,' said Sylvie. 'He was a very private person.'

Mary nodded. 'And you,' she asked tentatively, 'do you have anyone in your life?'

Sylvie twisted her fingers round the edge of her cup, not sure how much to say. 'There has been a man,' she said slowly. 'But he's married. I don't think I want to go on being the other woman. Waiting by the phone in case he is suddenly free—'

She stopped, unsure how much she could confide in Mary.

'Yes,' said Mary softly, 'that's hard. But sometimes that's all we have to make do with.'

8

Joe was worried. Against expectations the spell of warm weather had not brought new customers to the sauna, they seemed to prefer standing around the streets, where the bars spilt over onto narrow footpaths. When he'd persuaded Spencer to invest in the venture he'd assumed he was putting up his own money, rather than coming out of the reserves of the Global AIDS Trust. Spencer had assured him that the money was safe, but Joe had begun to wonder. Joe had barely known Pomfrey, but he guessed that he had been unaware that Trust funds were involved. He knew that when Pomfrey checked into the sauna, the night of his death, he had asked whether Joe was around, and it was only by chance that at the time he was picking up an order of souvlaki round the corner for the guys on duty. Now he would never know what Pomfrey might have wanted from him.

Joe had been reluctant to allow any drugs to pass through the sauna, but one of his silent investors had been persuasive. By using the sauna to pass on small quantities of crystal meth—only the best, he was assured—there would not only be an added cash flow, but the sauna itself would attract new customers. 'And cops,' grumbled Joe, but he felt he had no choice.

To save money Joe now spent several evenings at the front desk.

He rarely left before eleven, which only aggravated the already tense situation with his girlfriend. He'd lived with Nell for two years and maybe it was now time to call it quits. She was in her mid-thirties, ten years younger than him, and he sensed she was getting restless. Nell was anxious to have a child, a prospect that terrified him, as did any thought of permanence. Joe was not attracted to men sexually, but he liked the sense of masculine camaraderie that he felt roaming through the sauna, where naked bodies shed all external signs of wealth and privilege. Occasionally a patron would hit on him; he disabused them quickly, but he also felt a strange sense of flattery. It was not, however, something he talked about with his mates at the local Walthamstow pub.

Meanwhile he needed to check in on his business in Brighton. Maybe he'd take Nell down for a couple of nights, sleep over in his Bed and Breakfast, spend some time together. One of his main investors was in Brighton, he could use the opportunity to talk him into extending his holdings in the sauna. In which case maybe it was better to go alone; Joe was determined that Nell should have no idea of the details of his business, even more now that he was thinking of splitting up.

'Yes,' said Nell bitterly, 'that's typical. Shoot down to Brighton in the middle of summer and leave me here to swelter.'

'It's barely twenty degrees,' said Joe. 'You'll hardly swelter.'

'That's not the point.' Nell felt a surge of anger, as much with herself as with Joe. 'I know you don't want me with you.'

'It's business, doll. I'm not going to Brighton to lie around on the beach.'

'But I could enjoy the sun. While you do whatever shady business you have down there.'

She suddenly sounded angry. 'And what about that long weekend you promised me on the beach at Normandy? The problem with you Joe, is you're all talk and no action.'

'Brighton is work,' he said stonily. 'I don't want you getting involved in my business. Maybe it's good for us both if we have a bit of a break.'

Nell gulped but held back. 'OK,' she said, 'maybe. Maybe I won't be here when you get back.'

Joe looked at her, then turned and left the room. So this is how it ends, he thought, mutual indifference and then recriminations. Nell had been a good companion and a better bed mate, but Joe was hardly romantic enough to cling to a relationship past its natural ending. When a relationship became too much work his instinct was to cut it off and move on. Sorting out the finances of the sauna seemed more pressing and less emotionally taxing.

CB

A few days after her outing with Noel, Sylvie met Caitlin for a drink at a small bar near Covent Gardens. They had known each other for several years through Pomfrey's work and fell into that grey zone between being good acquaintances and close friends, but, thought Sylvie, Caitlin was the only person with whom she could share her reactions to Pomfrey's death. Like others working on the HIV Vaccine Project, Caitlin had been shocked at his sudden death, and vaguely discomforted when she was told that his cremation would be private, with a memorial to follow some unspecified time in the future.

Caitlin was dressed in a peasant peplum blouse, a riot of purples, yellow and peach; Sylvie looked comparatively severe in a pleated skirt with a simple off-white top. They exchanged air-kisses and ordered their drinks; a gin fizz for Sylvie, a negroni for Caitlin.

'I liked Pomfrey,' said Caitlin, once they had settled into their uncomfortable but elegant seats in a tiny booth and exchanged pleasantries. 'Of course, I didn't know him like you did.'

Sylvie nodded. Yes, she thought, in some ways I knew more about him than did his wife. The thought made her sad, perhaps she could have slowed him down in that last month when the demands of the Conference became crazy, maybe made his death less likely.

'I started to work for him by accident,' said Sylvie. 'I'd done a standard Arts degree, and had a couple of casual jobs, but then I went back and did a diploma in public relations, and there was a call for someone to help with an early AIDS fund raiser. That's where I first met Pomfrey—and when he started the Trust he asked me to work in the office. He had a personal assistant then, someone from the University, but when the Trust grew, and set up its own offices, he decided he needed someone full time to back him up there. I was just one of thousands of nice middle-class girls with lots of education and no career. I am so grateful for what I learnt working with Pomfrey.'

'He was easy to work for,' said Caitlin, 'much easier than Alejandro.' She thought for a moment. 'They both care of course. But Alejandro seems consumed by the idea of finding the vaccine.'

'I guess Pomfrey was more restrained. But he cared, he cared too much sometimes.' She sipped her drink, tempted to order a second. 'How did the two of them get on in the labs? Was there any tension between them?'

'Odd that you ask that,' said Caitlin. She thought back to that last memory, of Pomfrey looking flushed and Alejandro standing at the entrance to the animal house, a strange look on his face. 'I think so, but I'm not sure why.'

'They were both driven to find a vaccine,' said Sylvie. 'Do you think they were close?'

'Alejandro was very determined to trial the vaccine prototype on the monkeys,' said Caitlin. 'I think Pomfrey was less certain.' She looked at Sylvie. 'Do you think there's something suspicious about Pomfrey's death?'

'Suspicious?' Sylvie looked startled. 'It was sudden, of course. But people do have sudden heart attacks, and he was under a lot of stress. And he was diabetic.'

'I didn't know that,' said Caitlin. 'I never saw any signs—but I guess I wouldn't.'

Odd, thought Sylvie, that she hadn't known it until Mary mentioned it at the cremation. Not all diabetics, she knew, needed to inject themselves, but surely he would have said something. He had made comments about keeping his weight down, but that was hardly a sign of illness.

'We'll miss him on the project,' said Caitlin. 'I suppose Alejandro will take over running it—and I don't trust him. He's not as scrupulous as Pomfrey.'

'You care about your work, don't you?'

Caitlin nodded. 'My brother,' she said, 'he died just before the antiretrovirals became available. Such a horrible disease … I think that's what got me into this field and it's what keeps me going. That's why Pomfrey's death is so upsetting. If anyone could find a vaccine it was him.'

She blew her nose and looked at Sylvie.

'And you—what will you do now?'

Yes, thought Sylvie, that was the question. She felt deeply exhausted and wanted a break, an escape from the world of the Trust and the Conference in which she'd been immersed for the last few years. But there was something about Pomfrey's death that bothered her, and she knew she needed to figure it out before she made a definite move.

'I'm not sure,' she said, feeling the need to confide. 'I've been seeing a man for some time now—but he's married, and I think there's no future in it. Maybe I should leave London, look for a job in Europe perhaps, working with one of the big NGOs in Amsterdam or Geneva. Start afresh.'

Caitlin looked hard at her. 'Are you sure you weren't just a little in love with Pomfrey?' she asked.

'No,' said Sylvie. 'But he fascinated me more than anyone else I know.' She paused. 'And if I had been—he wasn't interested in me. Not that way at least.'

Caitlin looked at her curiously. 'You mean—?' She thought for a moment. 'Last year,' she said, 'there was a lab assistant. Young, good-looking, perhaps a little too eager. And Pomfrey seemed to take a lot of interest in him, he would always look for him and talk to him in a way he didn't with the others. Then one day the boy was gone, no explanation. I did wonder if something had happened.'

Pomfrey could be very judgmental, thought Sylvie, although courteous to everyone he met and slow to anger. But she had seen him lose his temper several times, and once he fell out with someone there was rarely a chance to reconcile. 'You don't happen to know the name of the assistant who vanished, do you?'

Caitlin looked at her curiously. 'I could find out,' she said. 'Is it important?'

'I don't know.' Why, Sylvie wondered, did she feel this urge to find out more about Pomfrey now he was dead. 'Probably not. But I worked with the man for three years. Maybe I just feel I need to understand him before I can let go.' She thought back to that moment in his office, when he had declared his love for Noel, never to be mentioned again. 'Perhaps I owe him that.'

☙

Rahid came out of the tube in Paddington and walked through the evening rush, tourists crowding around the pubs and money changers that lined Praed Street. As usual the streets were littered with the refuse of disposable living, and Rahid grimaced as he skirted past the remnants of a half-eaten hamburger. He opened the door of his flat, a small one-bedroom apartment hidden at the back of an old white terrace house and sniffed: there was a slight hint of marijuana in the air, suggesting Justin had only recently gone out. Rahid was torn between relief and anxiety; Justin was absent more and more often, and less inclined to talk about where he went.

Rahid grabbed a soda from the fridge and went into the small living area, flicking on the television as he did. It was a habit he'd slipped into since living with Justin, who watched seemingly incessant reruns of *Absolutely Fabulous*. Annoyed, Rahid turned off the set and put on a Keith Jarrett CD.

Now that Pomfrey no longer headed up the labs, he wondered whether he could re-submit his doctorate. The last few months of his candidature, when Pomfrey accused him of fudging results, still rankled and he thought that with a few modifications the thesis could be re-examined. That might mean asking Alejandro to become his de facto supervisor. He had met Alejandro during his time working as a research assistant in the laboratories, but they had rarely spoken. And he remembered seeing him when he visited the sauna to check up on their ongoing behavioral surveys, a little surprised that he would take such a personal interest. He would ring on Monday and make an appointment to see him.

9

'I could murder that woman,' muttered Alejandro. He was standing on the tennis court, his legs strangely white and muscular, waiting for his doubles partner who was engaged in an apparently fascinating conversation with one of the other members. With the approach of Wimbledon there was growing speculation about the Williams sisters, and whether they might end up playing each other in the finals, although the one Australian member of the club held a torch for Lleyton Hewitt.

'He plays with such single mindedness,' said Lucy, the oldest member of the club, who was sitting beside Caitlin, waiting for their match to be called. 'I think he plays to forget.'

Caitlin looked at her. 'To forget—?'

'Oh my dear, don't you know?' Lucy leant forward, her body tense with excitement. 'It's his son. Of course we shouldn't talk about it, but I happen to know he's been in and out of several rehab clinics. I think he's back in one now, somewhere in East London, I believe.'

Alejandro was bouncing a couple of balls with growing impatience. Tennis was his only relaxation, the one time when he thought neither about his research or his son. Several weeks ago Carlos had agreed to admit himself to a rehabilitation centre, and Alejandro had visited him there two nights before the Conference, the night of Pomfrey's death. Alejandro knew the centre well, as it was cooperating in HIV research with a number of venues, including the Spartacus Sauna. His wife was too upset by their son's frequent relapses to visit him; above all, she feared for their reputation if it became known that one of the country's leading medical researchers had a son who was an addict.

'Sorry.' His partner bounded onto the court, slightly out of breath. 'Held up. But ready to go, what?'

The four players walked to the net, tossed for first service. Alejandro was the first to receive, and Caitlin noted his stance, his body tensed forwards ready to leap at the ball. He was an impulsive player, quick to leap at any opportunity, sometimes cutting off his partner in the process.

'I wonder,' said Caitlin 'You don't happen to know which clinic his son is in?'

'Not really dear,' said the woman regretfully. 'Somewhere near Shoreditch I think, nowhere I would ever be likely to go.'

ଓ

Every second month Noel would spend most of Saturday at the book and stamp fair in the dank basements off Charing Cross. This was the only day he drove—Mrs Mackie having arranged for him to borrow an old van to carry books to and from the fair—and he steered carefully through the congested streets down to the Embankment. Outside the building a couple of determined stall holders were puffing on their last cigarettes before going in to set up. Noel parked and carried in three boxes, the usual assortment of thrillers, military histories and self-help books that seemed to do well at the fair.

Up to sixty stalls stretched in rows under the low cross-beamed ceilings, offering stamps, coins and, alongside Noel, several booksellers. He nodded to his neighbour, a rotund moustachioed man who specialised in secondhand children's books—Enid Blyton; complete sets of the William and Biggles stories—and settled in for the morning. The bulk of the customers were stamps and coin collectors, mainly middle-aged men in brown and green corduroys and check shirts, some of them specialised collectors, others clearly novices, willing to spend hours ferreting through cardboard boxes of loose stamps searching for anything that looked attractive.

He and the children's bookseller had an agreement to mind each other's stands if one needed to wander off, and after a couple of hours Noel went in search of coffee from the makeshift café at the other end of the hall. He stopped to say hello to one of the stamp dealers whom he knew from the Camden Markets, a specialist in British colonies, when he recognised the customer leaning over the stall.

'Hey!' he said 'Rahid?'

Rahid turned, looked momentarily startled, then smiled tentatively. 'Hello,' he said. 'You again.'

Noel nodded. 'I wouldn't have picked you for a stamp collector.'

'I'm not.' Rahid nodded to a couple of carefully mounted sheets of stamps on the counter. 'My Dad had some old stamps from Mauritius. He asked me to find out if they were worth anything.'

Most of the stamps were small squares with different images of Queen Victoria, several overprinted to show a change in currency from pennies to rupees. The dates, neatly written underneath each stamp, were all 1878/9.

The dealer sighed. 'If this were a complete set I could offer you a decent sum. But the ones that are missing—they're the ones that really have some value.'

'My Dad could do with the money,' said Rahid. 'What are they worth?'

'OK.' The dealer thumbed through his catalogue. 'I can give you twenty-five quid,' he said. 'It's hard to sell incomplete sets.'

Rahid pocketed the money and turned to Noel. 'So,' he said, 'you still trying to find someone who might have seen the Prof. that night?'

'I have a lead,' said Noel. 'The guy who was cleaning the rooms—named Winston. But he's left the sauna and I don't know how to find him.'

Rahid thought for a moment, wondering how much he was willing to share.

'Please,' said Noel, 'do you know the guy?'

'I heard,' said Rahid carefully, 'that he might have moved to Brighton. The person who'd know is Joe, the guy who owns the sauna.'

Noel felt suddenly excited. 'Where would I find him?'

'You've probably seen him there,' said Rahid. 'He's usually around: a biggish guy, red hair. He'll probably know what happened to Winston.'

Noel returned the van to Islington, stopping on the way to pick up a frozen shepherd's pie with a dutiful green salad, which he ate quickly before going out again. He shared a large, if old-fashioned, flat in the back of a three-storey yellowish stock-brick terrace, looking out on a small garden that was framed by several large geranium bushes. As part of his share of the lease Noel kept the garden neat; he had attempted a herb plot, but neighbourhood cats had dug it up. His flatmate worked in a nearby hospital and her shifts meant they rarely coincided, though it also meant Noel had the sense of being a temporary lodger who might be displaced at any moment were Emily to ask him to leave. But his room looked out onto the garden, and was bright, despite—perhaps because of— the rather garish green and white wallpaper left behind by previous owners.

Pomfrey's death had made him think about his life in new ways, to ask whether he was content to continue drifting. He had a job he liked, but one that would come to an end were Mrs Mackie to die, or to accept the inevitable decline of the used book trade. He had a few friends, none of them close; a sister and brother back in Newcastle, whose lives seemed so unlike his that only the artificial festivities of Christmas or his mother's birthday could preserve the illusion of family. He had only one serious relationship to look back on before he'd met Pomfrey, one that had ended in tears and bitterness, and made him wonder whether he would spend the rest of his life alone.

Peter had been almost exactly his age, and Noel had felt uneasy with his friends, who were more political and more outgoing than he. They liked to go to dance parties and drag shows, both of which made Noel feel uncomfortable. When Noel first discovered the gay world of London he'd enjoyed uncomplicated hook-ups, but he struggled with Peter's insistence that theirs should be an open relationship, and he realised that if it were to be serious he wanted a monogamous relationship. Meeting Pomfrey he sensed that an older man was safer, the very solidity of his career and marriage reassured him.

He had decided to follow Rahid's advice and look for Joe. This time Paolo at reception recognised him. But to Noel's query about meeting with Joe he rolled his eyes. 'Not here mate,' he said. 'Reckon he's gone down to Brighton for a couple of days.'

Noel persisted. 'Know where in Brighton?'

'Wouldn't have a clue. You could try his B & B, though.'

'He has one there?'

'Yeah.' Paolo ferreted around in a drawer. 'Here's a flyer for it: the *Prince Rupert*. Pretty poncy name, but reckon he'd stay there.'

The following day was a Sunday, which meant the bookshop would be shut for two days. He could go to Brighton overnight, maybe find somewhere close to Joe's B & B and contrive to run into him. His rather tattered gay guide listed a whole bunch of places where he might stay, grouped between St James Street and the sea. He picked one strategically close to Joe's *Prince Rupert*, though somewhat cheaper, and picked up the phone.

CB

As usual Caitlin and Rahid met outside a Scottish woollens shop near the British Museum, where they went for coffee. From a chance remark by Caitlin about her Scottish ancestry, the shop had become a shared reference, a totem of their friendship, which had begun in the labs and developed when they both attended the massive demonstrations against the Iraq War. Caitlin was an experienced demonstrator—her parents had marched for Vietnam —but for Rahid this was new: 'I resent the idea,' he told her, 'that my skin colour makes me a leftist.' He'd chosen biomedicine as a way of avoiding politics, but the rhetoric of Bush and Blair had turned him into a sporadic activist.

It was in conversations after the euphoria of that day, when almost a million people gridlocked central London, that they discovered a shared passion for classical music. Caitlin had studied the oboe before switching to virology; Rahid had first heard opera through recordings of Callas and Sutherland as a teenager and resented the assumption that as a third generation British Indian he should disavow western culture. They recognised a common urge for solitude that meant neither of them had been very successful in building long-term relationships, though Rahid had now moved in with someone he'd been seeing on and off for nine months.

'How's Justin?' said Caitlin.

'Justin?' said Rahid sardonically. 'Sometimes it seems he's more like a roommate than a lover.'

'So he's dating other guys?'

'Not exactly dating. Justin believes in direct action. He's hardly the monogamous type.'

'And that bothers you?'

'Not really. Guess we gays have a different concept of fidelity. If he likes to screw around that's his choice—as long as he plays safe.'

Caitlin looked hard at him, noticed the slight unease in his eyes as he half turned away from her. 'Perhaps,' she said. 'But jealousy is a pretty universal emotion.'

'I guess. But after all I do work in a gay sauna. You'd be amazed who I see coming in there.'

'Some of my girlfriends,' said Caitlin, sounding rather puzzled, 'tell me they wish there was a sauna for straight women, they're sick of hanging around bars and listening to a man's life story before anything happens. What Erica Jong called "a zipless fuck."' She shuddered: 'I can't imagine having sex with a stranger, not getting to know them first, maybe not even knowing their name.'

'Rahid,' she asked, changing the subject abruptly, 'do you remember the lab technician—think his name was Chris—who worked with Prof. Lister for a while, then disappeared one day? I think he might have been gay.'

He thought for a moment. 'Blonde guy, swimmer's build? Sure, I know Chris. Think he hangs out with the leather crowd, goes to bars like Central Station and the Fort.'

'Ever come to your sauna?'

'Possibly, we have leather nights there. Yeah, he might have been there a couple of times. Why are you asking?'

'I remember I was puzzled why he left us. He seemed to be getting on so well, then suddenly he wasn't there. Do you think he fell out with Prof.?'

'Possibly,' said Rahid, 'Lister wasn't the easiest guy to work with. All charm and manners until you crossed a line, then he could come down on you hard.'

'You hated him didn't you?'

'I admired him. That's what made it so hard—the kick in the guts. When he accused me of fudging my results and there was no more room for me in the Project. Yeah, guess I did hate him.'

He hesitated, not sure how far he could trust Caitlin.

'I saw him, you know, the night he died. He came to the sauna, was looking for Joe, the owner. But I didn't speak to him.' He swirled his spoon around his already empty cup, prospecting for the last bitter drops.

'Well,' said Caitlin, noticing how tense mention of Pomfrey made him. 'There are two operas opening next month that we might go to. Donizetti or Puccini?'

'Sounds like an Italian menu,' said Rahid. 'But *Lucia* every time!'

'Either way,' said Caitlin ruefully, 'it's the woman who gets screwed.' But it was a standard complaint, and she knew Rahid would dismiss it.

10

Though they left London for Brighton within an hour of each other, Joe and Noel travelled in different ways. Joe drove, cursing the traffic and the government that had yet to build a proper motorway. Noel made his way to Victoria Station, got lost trying to work out the right platform, and settled into a half-empty second-class carriage. He liked the slight motion of the train and the vista of suburbs, airport, countryside it traversed, until the flat Sussex Downs gave way to hillocks and housing estates that proclaimed the trip was nearing its end. His carriage was at the very end of the platform, and he walked slowly towards the exit, wondering why he had come and tempted to leap back onto the train and the safety of returning home. A couple of seagulls swooped low over the open platforms, and he jumped, startled, but suddenly determined to continue.

The bed and breakfast he had chosen was an old Regency terrace, now showing its age as if it were slowly sinking into irrelevance. A hand-painted sign proclaiming *The Brigadoon* flapped on top of a small set of steps leading up to a bright orange front door. Noel rang the bell and was greeted by a largish man, with balding ginger hair, and dressed in a flowing caftan. 'Well hello,' he said, shaking Noel's hand vigorously. 'I'm Maurice. Welcome to our home away from home.'

He escorted Noel up a narrow staircase to a small room, dominated by a large iron-posted bed and an ancient wooden wardrobe, but looking out, as Maurice stressed, onto a quiet if miniature square, neatly fenced with iron railings. 'If you lean out,' he said encouragingly, 'you can just get a glimpse of the pier.'

Noel decided to walk down to the beach and check out Joe's rather more luxurious B & B on the way. It was late afternoon, but already several pubs seemed full, patrons flowing onto the narrow pavements. Joe's *Prince Rupert* was closer to the Parade, a similar Regency style building to his accommodation, but in much better condition, with window boxes punctuating the facade of the house with bursts of yellows and purples.

Now that he was here, Noel realised he couldn't simply walk up to the building and ask for Joe; far better to contrive a way to run into him accidentally. Perhaps if he hung around he would see him, or at least manage to start a conversation with someone who could lead him to him. He'd noticed a small café at the corner of the street where he could sit and watch who came and went. The café was small and somewhat dingy-looking, but there was a minute outside table with a rather rickety chair, and Noel decided he could sit there and read his way through several slow coffees. After almost an hour, when no-one seemed to have either entered or left the *Prince Rupert*, he left and set off in the direction of the pier.

Tattered clouds covered the sky, but even when the sun broke through the sea stayed a tepid green, a flat expanse stretching towards France, small wavelets lapping the pebbles on the beach, where a few determined sun-bathers lay stretched out as if in supplication. Noel walked under the pier and along the foreshore, where various small galleries and produce shops huddled under arches, and squalls of seagulls bickered over discarded scraps. Noel had stopped to buy a carton of chips, when he noticed a tall young man with a carefully trimmed mohawk leaning against one of the stall fronts and licking a multi-coloured ice-cream. Unlikely, thought Noel, even as he looked at the man; but before he could summon up the nerve to accost him the man was joined by another, younger, more muscled and with shorter hair, who gave him a quick peck on both cheeks. They were about to move off when mohawk man noticed Noel staring at him.

'Hey,' he said, 'all okay man?'

Noel gulped. 'Yes. That is—you aren't Winston by any chance?'

'Nah,' said the man. 'Bobby. You looking for Winston?'

'You know him? About your age, same hairdo.'

'Might have seen him around,' said the man. 'Don't know where you'd find him though. Try the clubs round the Steyne maybe.'

'Thanks,' said Noel. 'Thank you.'

The two men nodded and walked off towards the city. Noel retraced his steps back towards his B & B, when he saw someone who was presumably Joe leaving the *Prince Rupert*. He decided to follow him, maybe he would lead him to Winston. If not, maybe he could find a way of talking to him, asking him directly if he knew Pomfrey and had seen him in the sauna.

Joe—yes; Noel was sure that was him—walked briskly past the wedding cake Royal Pavilion and up the slope towards the Lanes, Noel following, dodging the summer tourists. At the foot of the Lanes, a bewildering patchwork of shops selling a vast array of unnecessary goods, Joe entered a café, considerably smarter than the one where Noel had previously sat. Almost instantly he was joined by a tall man wearing clearly expensive designer jeans and jacket who led him to a table by the open window. With some nervousness Noel realised that were he to perch on the stools that ran alongside the edge of the café he could eavesdrop on their conversation.

Noel still carried a book with him, as he did from habit on every outing, and he could prop up Edmund White's *Boy's Own Story* against the window while sipping his coffee—a soy latte this time, with a Portuguese tart—and listen to the two men. But almost as soon as he had installed himself, carefully balancing book, coffee cup and cake on the narrow window ledge, he realised how absurd this was, as if he were playing a role in a bad spy melodrama. Wanting to extricate himself he stood up and knocked over his coffee, spilling it onto the sweater of the man he assumed was Joe.

'What the hell—!' Joe jumped up, startled, and turned on Noel.

'Sorry,' said Noel. 'Sorry,' he repeated, looking for napkins to wipe off the stains.

'No big deal,' said Joe.

Noel took a breath. 'You're Joe, aren't you?'

'Do I know you?'

'Sorry, I just thought … I was trying to find you. It's about the sauna.'

Joe's expression remained fixed, but he felt a new tension in his shoulders. 'What about it?'

'I was wondering—sorry, this is a bit of a wild stab—but did you know Pomfrey Lister? I think he was there about ten days ago.'

Joe frowned. 'Lister?—nah, sorry mate. Doesn't ring a bell.' He turned away from Noel. 'Good to meet you mate, but we're kind of busy here.'

'Of course … sorry again …' Noel left in a flurry of apologies, but he'd noticed Joe's expression change when he mentioned Pomfrey.

'What was that about?' asked Joe's companion. 'Who's he looking for?'

'Not sure,' said Joe. 'Probably a missing boyfriend.' But why, wondered Joe, and who was this guy who seemed to have tracked him down. He realised that he should have got his name, but it was not a conversation he wanted to prolong in front of one of his major backers. His task now was to keep Lou enthused about the sauna.

'We get all types coming to Spartacus,' he said confidently. 'I've had a couple of wives trying to find out if their husbands are there, shows we're really getting out there with our branding. What we need now is to improve the facilities, put in a bar and a café, that way the punters see it as somewhere to spend a whole evening and they come to us rather than those pissy bathhouses across the river.'

His companion looked at him. 'Maybe,' he said carefully, 'we need to increase the amount of—shall we say, goodies—that are available.'

'We have to be careful.' Joe frowned. 'Important we don't let word get out to the wrong people.'

'And you think it has?'

Uneasily Joe remembered Pomfrey asking for him the night he died and wondering what he might have known. 'I think,' he said carefully, 'we have to take precautions if it does.'

ℭ

'Hey,' said Justin, who was making dinner that evening and idly leafing through a stack of magazines with one eye on the stove. 'This professor of yours, the one who carked it in the sauna. This him?' He pointed to a small photograph accompanying a hastily written obituary article in the latest *New Scientist*.

Rahid nodded.

'I think I knew him,' said Justin thoughtfully. 'He came into the *Backstreet* when I was working there—I remember him, because he never got into the action. He'd stand by the bar in full leather, sipping a beer and watching, always watching as if he expected something to happen. But it never did.'

'You ever speak to him?'

'I did, one night. Said there were plenty of guys in the bar who'd fancy a daddy type like him. He said he enjoyed hanging out and it would shock his wife if she knew. Seemed as if he was almost daring her to find out.'

'That doesn't make sense.'

'I think he was just being smart—and letting me know he was married. Like I said, he never seemed to make contact with anyone.'

Rahid wondered whether this threw any light on Pomfrey's death, it certainly suggested his was not a happy marriage.

'Apparently he'd come to the sauna a couple of times before that night,' said Rahid thoughtfully. 'But I never saw him.'

'Maybe he came to scare Joe,' said Justin scornfully. 'Not that it would be hard.'

Rahid looked at him quizzically. 'You know Joe?' he asked.

'Nah. But a couple of mates were talking about him last night, because they'd been to the sauna, looking to score. Reckon they knew him from hanging round the pub in Newington Green. He had a reputation for a big mouth, but it was all bluster—he'd pick a fight and as soon as anyone confronted him he'd duck for cover.' He looked hard at Rahid. 'Hey, you scared of him?'

'Course not, but he's my boss. He could fire me any time.'

'Doubt it,' said Justin cheerfully. 'You know too much.'

He grabbed the frying pan from the stove and started ladling out something that had a vague resemblance to the beef stroganoff his grandmother used to cook.

'Here,' he said, 'come and eat.'

There was a short silence as he dished out the meal onto mismatched plates. But Justin was intrigued.

'So,' he asked, 'why do you think the Prof. was in the sauna that night anyway? You think he was after some action?'

Rahid thought a moment. 'I'm not sure,' he said slowly. 'It was leather night—and you said you'd seen him in leather? Never talked to him?'

'Not really.' Justin grinned. 'Want me to see what I can find out about his exploits?'

'Yeah. I've met someone who claims to have been his lover—but he didn't strike me as the leather type. Maybe Prof. Lister was cheating on him as well as his wife.'

He wondered whether Alejandro knew about Pomfrey's leather evenings; he knew there had been tension between the two of them. The question, he thought, was how he might make use of that knowledge.

ෆ

'So,' said Alejandro 'You wish to resume your doctorate?'

They were sitting together in his research office, little more than a furnished cubicle adjoining the laboratories. Alejandro sat behind a small desk, crammed with a computer and random files; behind him a large whiteboard showed signs of earlier calculations and test results. The only personal note was a small calendar showing masterpieces from the Uffizi on the back of the office door.

'Technically,' said Rahid, 'I never suspended. But there was a problem with submitting my thesis—Professor Lister refused to sign off on it.'

Alejandro leant back on his chair and looked hard at Rahid. 'I recall,' he said, 'there was some question of you fudging—or at least massaging—the results of your experiments?'

'But I didn't!' Rahid was indignant, struggling to keep his voice level. 'He never gave me the opportunity to explain.'

'I see,' said Alejandro. 'Of course we can't ask him. Perhaps you might explain exactly what it was you proposed to clarify.'

Rahid took out a small folder of graphs and tables. Twenty minutes later Alejandro was sufficiently impressed to agree to read the full thesis and look for new examiners if he deemed it appropriate.

Rahid breathed a quiet sigh of relief. His hunch that Alejandro would skirt over the slight discrepancy that had alerted Pomfrey had proved correct.

'Other than that,' Alejandro asked carefully, 'what did you make of Pomfrey?'

Rahid paused. 'His research,' he said carefully, 'was exciting. I think he might have been on a breakthrough towards an HIV vaccine.'

'Indeed.' Alejandro coughed. 'Indeed. But of course, it was a team effort. Pomfrey was perhaps too inclined to take all the credit. Do you think that was behind his falling out with you?'

'No.' said Rahid. 'It was because my results contradicted his. When I showed him what I'd discovered he got very angry and that's when things started to unravel.'

'Of course,' Alejandro said, 'I can't take sides in what happened. But I shall look at your findings very carefully.' He stood up and carefully shut the office door, giving Rahid a small smile. 'I think,' he said complacently, 'we may be on the verge of a very exciting breakthrough here. My work has diverged a little from the lines Pomfrey was pursuing. But now I shall be able to get on with it more easily.'

He looked hard at Rahid. 'I'm assuming I can trust you not to repeat this,' he said, lowering his voice. 'I think Pomfrey was possibly sabotaging my research and your results would have supported the lines I was following. But finding the vaccine is too important for any one person to stand in the way.'

Rahid smiled. 'Of course' he said. 'I look forward to working with you, Professor Herrera.'

11

'Arabella, my love?'

Spencer was stretched out on the leather sofa (*Darlings of Chelsea*), idly flicking through the Sunday papers. Arabella was seated across the room, casually dressed in sweatpants and a multi-coloured top (*Belles of London*), idly flicking through a couple of magazines.

'Just wondered ... Has anyone said anything to you about Pomfrey? About his death, I mean?'

'No,' said Arabella, not particularly interested. 'Other than surprise that the funeral happened so quickly—but I assume that was to get it out of the way before your precious Conference.'

'You haven't been in touch with Mary?'

'I don't think Mary approves of me. Didn't you suggest it would be better were I not to come to the cremation? Of course, I wrote to her when I heard of his death—you did get your assistant to send flowers from us? But I think Mary was always a little jealous of me.'

'What do you mean?'

'She clearly liked you, Spencer. If she wasn't such a frump I could have resented it. But you did spend time together.'

Spencer swallowed uneasily. 'Business,' he said, 'purely business. Things we didn't necessarily share with Pomfrey.'

Arabella didn't add that she had long ago given up feeling resentment at Spencer's flirtations. Instead she carefully folded her magazine and looked at him.

'The night Pomfrey died,' she said. 'Where were you?'

'Wasn't I at home?'

'No, you had taken the car out after dinner. The next thing I knew was you coming home very late with a story about being called to help move his body—how did they know where to find you?'

Spencer tapped his titanium-cased mobile. 'You know I never go anywhere without this. Joe rang me.'

'But what were you doing that evening?'

Spencer looked flustered. 'Not sure,' he said. 'Errands—so many loose ends to tie up before the Conference—had to check in on a couple of our sponsors. Now, of course, we have the future of the Trust to worry about. I'm worried what the Trustees might do—they refuse to commit to a successor to Pomfrey. Elvira Blomvquist wants to come into the office and go through the accounts.'

'The Norwegian woman? Grey hair and sensible shoes?'

'And one of the top people in her field. Not someone to have offside.'

Arabella stretched, throwing her magazines onto the floor. 'Well maybe we should invite her to a small dinner. Impress her with some of *our* top people.' She looked hard at Spencer.

'Should you be worried?' she asked.

'No,' he said, but Arabella knew he was lying. When she first met Spencer she had thought him the most charming man she'd ever come across and had fallen in love. In time she had come to recognise that his charm was the product of total egotism, and a need to be in control, which he was very skilled at hiding.

'As long as she's not a forensic accountant,' said Spencer. 'Much easier now Pomfrey's out of the way. If the Conference makes a profit there will be nothing to worry about.'

೧೮

That Sunday evening in Brighton Noel felt very alone. His approach to Joe had backfired; even if he could find Winston it was likely that would be no more successful. He'd walked back from the Lanes through crowds of excited tourists, who were spilling over into bars and restaurants, leafing through postcard stands along the edge of the Royal Pavilion, and stopped briefly at a secondhand bookshop, not finding anything of interest. Back in his B & B he took refuge in his book. Around seven, the sun having come out from the clouds so that his room was uncomfortably warm, he wandered up to St James Street and found a small Polish café where he ordered a plate of pierogi, which came smothered in red cabbage and, presumably as a nod to British tastes, smashed peas. There were a couple of gay bars in the immediate area, and he wandered up and down the street, no longer sure what he was looking for.

He was standing disconsolately outside what seemed to be a very crowded disco, strobe lights and loud music blaring out onto the narrow footpath, when there was a peremptory tap on his shoulder.

'You,' said Joe. 'You're the bloke who spilt coffee on me, right?'

Startled Noel pulled back, almost knocking over two women in what seemed a deep domestic row outside the disco.

'Yes,' he said. 'Sorry.'

'You said you were looking for me? What's your name mate?'

Noel gulped. 'Noel,' he said. 'And I thought maybe you knew him—Pomfrey Lister, that is. Maybe you'd seen him at your sauna?'

'I might have.' Joe made a hasty calculation just how much this bloke might know. 'What's your angle, mate?'

'I think he was there the night he died,' said Noel. 'I just want to know if that's the case.'

Joe shook his head. 'Can't help you there, mate. You saying someone died in my sauna?'

'No.' Noel took another step back. 'No, it's just that he died very suddenly. And maybe he'd been there that night—I mean, not that there's really a connection—just that I'd feel better if I knew.'

Joe looked hard at him. 'Better not to ask too many questions,' he said, 'they can only get you into trouble.'

He punched Noel lightly on the arm and walked away in the direction of the Parade.

But he did know, thought Noel, and he doesn't want me to know. All the more reason, he told himself, walking up the street towards the next corner bar, to find Winston.

'Home early?' Maurice was tidying the hallway and beckoned Noel into a small over-furnished front room, loaded with slightly fading chintz furniture and a mantelpiece bearing a crowded collection of assorted beach souvenirs. 'Can I offer you a drink?'

'Well—' said Noel, uncertain, but Maurice was already reaching for a large crystal decanter. 'Home brewed elderberry wine,' he said, pouring out two generous amounts. 'You look as if you need cheering up.'

Noel made a face. 'Perhaps,' he said. 'Maybe I'm not sure why I came to Brighton.'

'Ah,' said Maurice, 'but you're looking for someone? A boyfriend perhaps?'

'No. Just a bloke who used to work at the Spartacus sauna in London.'

Maurice winked. 'Naughty boy,' he said. 'And you have a thing for this boy?'

'I think he might be able to help me,' said Noel, suddenly eager to talk. About Pomfrey, about the shock of his death, about seeing his car at the sauna and his growing need—obsession, perhaps—to know whether that's where he spent the last evening of his life, about being accosted by Joe, and the futile search for Winston, whom he thought was somewhere in Brighton …

'Then,' said Maurice firmly, 'we can find him. Let me ask around. You know nothing about this guy except the description and he's called Winston?'

Noel nodded. 'But I have to return to London tomorrow,' he said. 'No further along.'

'Give me a week,' said Maurice. 'Come back next weekend—as my guest. You can even come and watch the Brighton Wilde Players rehearse. We're doing *The Importance of Being Earnest*.

We're an amateur group, mainly older poofs—I play Miss Prism. The governess.'

Noel retreated to his room with the uneasy feeling that maybe Maurice was hitting on him but reassured that there still might be a chance of finding Winston. He rather dreaded descending for breakfast the next morning, but luckily there were others in the small dining alcove—three hearty German backpackers who seemed very amused to find themselves in a gay B & B—and Maurice was totally occupied serving the full English breakfast on which he prided himself. Shaking off the aftertaste of bacon and sausage, Noel made his way to the station and the return to London.

12

The offices of the Trust were near Russell Square, in a four-storey terrace house originally built by the Cubitt brothers. After a couple of days break the staff spent the rest of the week moving papers and computers from the Conference venue back to their offices, and it was here that Elvira called on Spencer.

Spencer was not in that morning, having decided it would be politic to accompany two of the departing trustees to Heathrow. Sylvie, however, was.

It was a crisp summer morning and they sat outside a nearby café, perched on slightly rickety chairs, sipping their coffees.

'It must be hard for you,' said Elvira. 'Will you stay on now that Pomfrey is no longer with us?'

Sylvie nodded. She wasn't ready to share her doubts about her future with someone who was essentially a stranger.

'Did Pomfrey ever suggest he was concerned about the finances of the Trust?'

'He was worried, I know that. But he didn't confide in me what exactly was troubling him.'

'You see,' said Elvira, 'The Trust has a rather strange structure. Because Pomfrey founded it, and brought in the funds to get it going, he also kept more control than is usual for a board president. We just aren't sure how much the Trust has in its accounts, and now he's dead only Spencer knows that.'

'Yes,' said Sylvie. 'I know that Spencer acted as financial officer as well as chief executive. Maybe not even Pomfrey knew the full story.'

'I know one of our main donors,' said Elvira, leaning forward. A small crumb of her muffin was on her chin, and Sylvie flicked at it with her handkerchief. 'Maybe our principal donor. Do you know the Baroness?'

Of course, Sylvie had heard of her. The Baroness von Hochmittelburg was a former English actress who had married a wealthy Austrian banker and now lived in semi-retirement in a village in the Tyrol. She had first met Pomfrey at an Alpine ski resort, shortly after he had begun researching hepatitis viruses, and they had remained in touch. Years later, after relatives of the Baroness died from AIDS in South Africa, she had offered to fund research into the epidemic, which became the basis for the Trust. On her insistence Pomfrey was to head the Trust until he chose to retire and could only be succeeded by someone she approved.

'But no,' she said, 'I never met her. She rarely leaves Austria I understand.'

Elvira sighed. 'Her health is uncertain. And she is a vain woman—she wants people to remember her as a great beauty, not a shrivelled old woman. But she remains determinedly English; I understand her servants are all expats and she speaks only minimal German, even though she's lived there for decades.'

'And she is our main donor?'

'Yes. But there are others. And the reality of a few big donors means that there is a certain amount of secrecy—when we asked Spencer about it he talked about the need to be discreet.' She snorted. 'That might mean anything.'

Sylvie nodded. 'I wondered,' she said tentatively, 'that is, I saw a couple of emails—after Pomfrey died, wasn't sure whether I should look at his messages or not—but he seemed concerned. There was a reference to a possible inquiry by Inland Revenue—but no details. And then I thought it was ghoulish to be reading messages from a dead man and I stopped reading his account.'

Elvira frowned. 'But this could be serious,' she said. 'And we need to sort it out before someone is appointed to replace Pomfrey.'

'There was something else,' said Sylvie, pleased to find someone with whom she could confide. 'There were a couple of messages coming from someone called Righteous. Pomfrey seemed worried about homophobic messages—that was something we dealt with in writing the Conference communique—'

'The communique adopted by the delegates at the closing ceremony?'

'Yes. Of course, we'd pre-written the text, but there were lots of meetings to polish it, and there was a deadlock between some of the community groups and the government delegates from Nigeria and Belarus. They were determined there should be no mention of homosexuals or drug-users in the document.'

Elvira sighed. 'Yes,' she said, 'I remember the arguments.' She looked at Sylvie. 'And you think Pomfrey was in touch with someone called Righteous? That's an odd name?'

'It's a Biblical reference,' said Sylvie. 'I looked it up and I found this in the *Book of Common Prayer*.' She reached for her handbag and took out a carefully folded scrap of paper. 'Here,' she said, *'For the rod of the ungodly cometh not into the lot of the righteous: lest the righteous put their hand unto wickedness.'*

'So what is this Book of Common Prayer?'

'I think it's the basic text for Anglican churches,' said Sylvie. 'We came across it at school, but I didn't pay much attention.'

'And Righteous?—does that term suggest anything to you?'

'Only that it's someone who is religious. And probably fervent. Someone who is working against our commitment to reach people most at risk of HIV.'

Elvira sighed. 'Yes,' she said, 'like the Catholic bishops who preach against condoms. Hardly surprising they would be sending messages to Pomfrey. The real question is whether there's a connection between this Righteous person and the money problems.'

'I don't know.' Sylvie frowned, trying to recall anything Pomfrey might have said that would help. 'The last couple of weeks there was so much going on—the Conference took over all our lives. I spent most of the time dealing with travel problems, I didn't see that much of him.'

She gulped, and swallowed the last dregs of her coffee, hit by the reality that he was dead. 'I wish I knew more. Maybe I could talk to Mary?'

'Yes ...' Elvira was surprisingly uncertain. 'Spencer thinks we should name her president of the Trust. I'm not sure—I know Alejandro wants it badly.'

Sylvie smiled. 'He wants a life peerage,' she said. 'I know that Pomfrey was in line for that, probably in the next honours list.'

'Let me meet with Spencer first,' said Elvira. 'We can talk again after that.'

She stood up. 'I'll walk you back to the offices—he may have returned by now.'

Spencer looked somewhat nervous as he saw the two women enter, but he greeted Elvira warmly. 'I understand you have some questions for me,' he said jovially. 'Only too happy to help.'

He led her into his office, a large room dominated by his desk, which was largely bare except for a few judiciously displayed photos, mainly of Spencer with various international celebrities. The Trust had been lent a suite of rooms on the ground floor, enough for Spencer and several assistants, and Spencer had taken some care in furnishing his office to offer the right mixture of assurance and taste. The upkeep was expensive, but Spencer liked to say that only the appearance of money attracted more money.

He pointed Elvira to a black leather armchair, strategically positioned to give a view over the nearby square.

'Can I be honest with you?' Spencer ferreted in the desk drawers for papers. 'Pomfrey didn't always keep me informed of some of the financial details. I think he may have invested some of our finances in ways that were unorthodox, to say the least. Now the Conference is over I'm trying to track this down.'

'So you think some money may have been used outside the agreed purposes of the Trust?'

'Not sure,' said Spencer, hoping his investments of Trust resources was sufficiently opaque to avoid her scrutiny. 'I do need some time—first we have to settle all the finances of the Conference, and that will take a few weeks at least. I'm sure you understand.'

Elvira nodded. 'I wonder,' she said, 'do you know anything about Righteous?'

'No,' said Spencer, suddenly tense. 'Is that an organisation?'

Elvira shrugged. 'I think it might be a person. But someone Pomfrey knew. Someone who was trying to derail our prevention work.'

'No,' said Spencer too emphatically. 'No idea. Where did you hear this?'

'The term came up ... maybe from Pomfrey?'

'Well,' said Spencer at his most persuasive, 'I wouldn't worry about it. Probably a fringe group—we hear from a lot of those. I'll ask around if you like.' He leaned over the desk towards her. 'Have you thought about a successor to Pomfrey yet? I was wondering whether the best tribute we could offer would be to ask Mary to take on the role.'

Elvira looked a little startled. 'But doesn't she run her own NGO? Wouldn't that be a conflict of interest?'

'Think of it as building a bigger movement,' said Spencer reassuringly. 'How about a small dinner with Mary before you leave London?'

13

'I've had it with men!' Sylvie had met up again with Caitlin, this time in a gourmet sandwich bar in Clerkenwell, having finally ended her relationship with Geoffrey in a couple of long and unsatisfactory phone conversations, and she wanted the solace of another single woman. Her sister, and her two 'best friends' from university—but what did that mean anymore?—were married, all with young kids, and she had always been reticent talking with them about her relationship with a married man.

Caitlin nodded sympathetically. Her own knowledge of relationships was somewhat limited, and she had begun to wonder whether she was perhaps asexual, having come across the term in an article about a new group founded in New York which claimed this as a distinct orientation. She could admire the beauty of certain men, but the idea of being naked, sweaty, their bodies joined together, rather repelled her. Most of her male friends, like Rahid, were gay, and if she was honest she would admit that she avoided overt lesbians, perhaps fearful they might hit on her.

'And I'm too old and jaded to go back into the bar scene,' said Sylvie ruefully. 'I need ways to meet men that are natural, not fuelled by alcohol and dim lighting.'

She took another bite of her pumpkin and feta frittata, which tasted surprisingly bland. She grabbed a sachet of mustard and squeezed out an unpalatable orangey blob.

'I don't suppose,' said Caitlin, 'that you play tennis? You might want to join my club?'

'I haven't played for years. Not since school—but I was quite good. Maybe I should take it up again.' She had a sudden flashback to her school, one of the best grammar schools in the Midlands, when life seemed far simpler than right now. Memories of afternoons on the tennis courts, of being bused across Manchester to compete in inter-school events, of her first crushes—she shook her head impatiently, resisting the temptation for nostalgia.

'That's where Alejandro plays, right?' She remembered her promise to Noel. 'Guess that would give me an opportunity to talk to him. I assume there are some younger single men as well?'

'There are a few. But I avoid them—they are super competitive. The club's a little way out—towards Richmond. But I could drive you.'

'OK,' said Sylvie. 'Next weekend perhaps.'

ᘓ

Sylvie was a little nervous as she waited for Caitlin. It was many years since she'd played seriously, and she wondered if she would measure up. She'd made a last-minute dash to Oxford Street to buy the right clothes, even though Caitlin had assured her the dress code was less rigid than it used to be. But it was a perfect summer day, and Caitlin cheered her up with gossip about Colin Firth, whose latest movie she'd seen the previous evening.

'Here we are,' said Caitlin, driving to the end of a suburban street, lined with solid two-storey houses and carefully curated gardens. She parked the car and led Sylvie up to the clubhouse, a low brick building, with a white concrete frieze edging the roof, where she introduced her to several of the Club committee, seated on the long veranda that encircled the club house. 'Always good to have a new woman player,' said Lucy, inspecting Sylvie as if she were an item for auction. 'We're very democratic here—we even have members who went to comprehensive state schools. I assume we should put you down for social rather than pennant?'

Sylvie nodded and was led off to a far court where a couple of young women and a spry older man were hitting balls enthusiastically, if not always accurately. Walking across to the court she noticed Alejandro in a spirited doubles match. It was strange, Sylvie thought, how little she really knew Alejandro. In the leadup to the Conference she had sat in many long meetings with him, had helped him construct the program for the scientific tracks, had even driven with him one gloomy evening to collect one of their plenary speakers from Gatwick. But their conversations had never gone beyond the organisational—once, she recalled, there had been a short discussion of the Blair government, but that had largely revolved around which ministers should be invited to speak.

After the match, in which Sylvie acquitted herself adequately, despite serving two double faults in the last set, they walked up to the clubhouse where tea and cake was on offer. Alejandro was in deep conversation with a couple of the players, but when he saw Sylvie he came over to her.

'You played well,' he said, with the tone he used with bright undergraduate students.

Sylvie nodded. 'Did you win?' she asked.

Alejandro beamed. 'We did,' he said. 'I take winning very seriously. And congratulations on the Conference by the way. I think it went off rather well, all things considered. We did Pomfrey proud. Of course, we were all very sad about his death. I had to certify it, you know.'

'Why did Mary call you? Surely he had his own doctor?'

Alejandro looked a little flustered. 'Yes, think she couldn't get hold of him—and thought it better to be discreet. After all, I do still practice.'

'Did you know he was diabetic?'

Alejandro looked a little surprised. 'No,' he said. 'But I did see heart medication by the bed. Of course, he'd been under a lot of stress, with the Conference about to open.

He nodded his head and turned away. 'Must go talk to the club secretary,' he said. 'Glad you've joined us.'

Later, when she thought back on the conversation, Sylvie was struck by the number of times she'd heard Pomfrey's stress emphasised. She had worked closely with him over the few weeks before the Conference and to her he'd seemed relaxed, despite the constant interruptions and rescheduling. If anything, he thrived on the challenges the Conference brought. 'Has anyone died?' he'd ask, chuckling, when another Conference hiccup occurred, reminding Sylvie that preventing people dying was the purpose of the Conference, a useful thought when they were besieged with visa delays, flight cancellations and plenary speakers who demanded hotel upgrades.

೦ಌ

Noel walked with Maurice along the foreshore away from the centre of Brighton, ending up in a large nineteenth century pub, a stolid off-white three-storey building overhung with ivy and honeysuckle. A small group of clearly local customers were drinking quietly in the front bar, but Maurice led him down a short passage to a back parlour, where about fifteen people were gathered, laughing, drinking, clearly a group who knew each other and met regularly. 'Sometimes it's karaoke,' whispered Maurice excitedly, 'but tonight it's trivial pursuit.'

A short woman with blue-tinged hair and wearing a purple pantsuit grabbed a microphone and called everyone to order. There were three or four tables set around the room, and people gravitated in groups of three or four; mostly, Noel noticed, older men, but there was one table of four women and standing quietly at the back was a younger man with a crewcut and slightly pitted skin. Dutifully Noel followed Maurice to a table close to the empty fireplace and was introduced to his companions.

'Team-mates,' said Maurice firmly, 'we are going to win this evening.'

The next forty minutes saw Maurice's team neck and neck with the table of women, though neither knew who had played Robin Hood in the original BBC television series, filmed in the year of the Coronation. At the break Noel claimed he needed fresh air and went into the street, mainly to escape the curiosity of the others at his table, and ran into the young man who was bent over trying to light a cigarette away from the breeze.

'Hello,' said Noel tentatively, 'I'm Noel.'

The man turned around and grinned. Noel saw that he was taller and younger than he'd realised, with a generous mouth and the wisps of a small moustache clinging to his upper lip.

'Jaz,' said the man. 'What gets you here with all these old queens?'

'I'm staying at *The Brigadoon*,' said Noel. 'Maurice's B & B. How about you?'

Jaz shrugged. 'I know a couple of the geezers,' he said airily. 'Done the odd job for them.' He looked carefully at Noel. 'You into daddies?'

'Daddies?'

'Older men, mate.'

Noel thought; was that how others might have seen his relationship with Pomfrey? He'd been aware of the age gap, that was something new for him, but he'd never considered it as defining his sexual tastes. Looking at Jaz, who had moved closer to him, he thought there was something exciting about a younger man, a man who—Jaz's arm was now brushing against him—was clearly interested in hooking up.

'I did love an older man,' he said carefully. 'But he's dead.'

'Sorry to hear that mate.' Jaz touched his cheek gently, and Noel shivered. 'Let's get out of here,' Jaz said.

'I—I can't. I came with Maurice.'

'So? You're not screwing him are you?'

'God no!' Noel thought. 'OK,' he said, 'but go where?'

'You like mangoes?'

'I'm not sure. I don't think I've ever had one.'

'Back at mine,' said Jaz casually. 'Something very sexy about eating a mango: licking the juice off your fingers …'

Jaz had a room in a Victorian terrace house, not very different to the one where Noel lived in London, but on a busy narrow street, barely wide enough for the double decker buses to pass. His room was dominated by a low double bed, neatly made, and a heavy wooden wardrobe, on top of which perched a half-finished Lego construction. The room was wallpapered with crimson and yellow, against which Jaz had stuck various posters, including several from leather bars and, Noel noticed, the Spartacus sauna. There was a sink in the corner of the room, and next to it a small fridge, on top of which sat a bowl with two shrivelled apples. Magazines, neatly stacked, were piled alongside the bed and a small television set was placed on a somewhat rickety stand.

'Here we go,' said Jaz, kicking off his shoes. He opened the fridge and took out two beers and a small carefully wrapped package. 'You want to puff? Think there's some weed and skins here.'

'I don't really—' said Noel nervously, but Jaz was already rolling a joint, and lay back on the bed, beckoning Noel to join him. 'Guess I was wrong about the mango,' he said, grinning. 'Finished it yesterday.'

Noel wasn't sure he was even attracted to Jaz, but he was very persuasive, and the sex, when it happened, was gentle more than passionate; Noel left promising to stay in touch. 'I'm up in London next week,' said Jaz and they made a tentative plan to get together for a drink. Noel returned to *The Brigadoon*, where Maurice seemed to have waited up for him, his mood a mixture of disapproval and prurience as he plied Noel with questions.

14

Back in London, Noel called Sylvie. She was somewhat reluctant to meet him but agreed to a coffee later that week.

'Nowhere too near the office,' she said. 'Let's meet at the National Portrait Gallery.'

Noel arrived early and walked through the Gallery, pausing, as usual, by the famous Westall portrait of Lord Byron. He rarely went to galleries, but when he did he was easily enthused, particularly when he found images of authors whose books he knew. Noel had always enjoyed reading, but now he worked in the trade he was learning about authors he'd assumed were out of his reach, and he was particularly captivated by the early nineteenth century romantics.

Sylvie was already in the café when he joined her, leafing through a morning newspaper which someone had left on the table. 'So,' she said, 'you went to Brighton?'

'I met Joe,' said Noel. 'Guy who owns the sauna. And I think he knows something.'

'Something?'

'I'm sure he knew who Pomfrey was—and he knew that Pomfrey was at the sauna the night he died.'

Sylvie looked hard at Noel. 'Why do you persist with this?' she asked. 'What difference would it make? He's dead, after all.'

'I know,' said Noel quietly. 'But he told me I was the only man he could imagine making love to. I just want to know that he meant it.' He sniffled back a tear. 'I hate the idea that he might have spent his last night with someone else.'

He finished his scone and grinned, somewhat sheepishly. 'I met someone in Brighton,' he said. 'He's coming up to London in a couple of days.'

C８

While he was waiting for clients in the small, airless massage room, Rahid would play music on an old Walkman that he had owned since undergraduate days. He kept a small stack of contemporary pop tapes to play for clients; when he was alone he would listen to early Verdi operas—*Nabucco*; *Ernani*; *Macbeth*—and use the time to reflect on his future. His family had treated his liking for classical music much as they would treat his homosexuality, with a mixture of incomprehension and strained tolerance.

Rahid had grown up in a lower middle-class suburb of Sheffield, and was an only child, a loner at school in part because he was academically ahead of almost all his peers. He recalled the geeky kid, who collected autographs and listened to classical music on his transistor radio, and recognised the ways in which he had changed, the gym work to build up his muscles and the growing determination to establish himself in the world of biomedicine that had led to first-class honours and then the scholarship to work on the frontline of virological research. His falling out with Pomfrey had been a blow, but he would find a way around that, whatever it took.

He was caught up in the final scene of *Macbeth* when Joe walked in, shutting the door behind him.

'Mate,' said Joe, 'do you know anything about this bloke who's been asking questions about Professor Lister? Noel, I think his name is.'

'Yeah,' said Rahid, 'he was here a week or so ago. But I didn't tell him anything.'

'Lister was here once before he died,' said Joe. 'Came in to look at that research project the University crew are doing. Then he came back—asked to see me—any idea why?'

'No.' Rahid thought. 'That was the night he died?'

'Later,' said Joe firmly. 'At home. You hear otherwise?'

'No,' said Rahid hastily. 'But you think he was onto us, boss?'

Joe looked hard at Rahid. 'I don't know what you mean, mate,' he said.

Rahid signalled that he was zipping his lips. Several times he'd been asked to give a small packet to clients after their massage, and he had a shrewd suspicion of what was in it. But if Joe wanted him to pretend ignorance that suited him.

'I've had nothing to do with Lister since I worked in his labs,' he said. 'Guess neither of us is going to be too upset if he's not around any longer.'

Joe nodded. 'Let me know if that bloke shows up again,' he said. 'Don't like loose ends.'

Back in his office he rang Spencer. 'We need to get our story straight, mate,' he said. 'Too many people around asking questions.'

C03

The following Saturday afternoon, Arabella and Noel were both in the Borough Markets, though unknown to each other. Arabella had stopped in to buy some charcuterie for the evening's dinner party and Noel had arranged to meet Jaz, who was taking the Brighton train to London Bridge. The bulk of the dinner would be catered, but Arabella liked to visit the produce stalls in the market to add a personal touch.

Jaz had been very precise about where they should meet—'By the oyster bar, mate,' he'd said on the phone, 'towards the back, near Stoney Street.' But Noel was nervous about finding it, and was twenty minutes early. He wandered around, struck by the colours and scents and sounds of the market, constantly looking at his watch so as to not miss Jaz.

And there he was: the same tall young man with the slightly crooked full mouth, and the closely cropped hair, wearing a t-shirt from the show *Queer as Folk*. 'Hey matey,' said Jaz, tapping him affectionately on the shoulder. 'So what's happening?'

Noel realised that his anticipation at seeing Jaz again had not meant thinking beyond their initial rendezvous. If this was a date he wasn't at all sure of the next move, but Jaz took control.

'Can we go back to your place?' he asked.

Noel hesitated: was that what he wanted? Would his flatmate be there and if so would she object?

'Perhaps later,' he said, temporising. 'Where are you staying?'

'Here to see my Mum,' said Jaz. 'She's over in Stoke Newington. But she doesn't expect me for hours.' He noticed Noel's anxiety and gave him a quick kiss. 'Could have suggested the Spartacus, mate,' he said. 'But that's off limits for me now.'

Noel looked startled. 'Why?'

'Used to work there,' said Jaz. 'Guess they'd rather I stayed away.'

They had almost walked to the northern edge of the Markets, the Gothic spires of Southwark Cathedral looming ahead of them. Noel pulled Jaz to a stop, took him by the shoulders.

'When was that?' he asked. 'When did you stop working at Spartacus?'

'Couple of weeks ago,' said Jaz. 'There was—there was an incident. And Joe, the owner, thought it better if I left. Helped me find a job in a pub down in Brighton and said he'd look after me if I decided to go back to college. Want to study photography, mate.'

'An incident?'

'Yeah. Some geezer passed out in a cubicle. Think he had a stroke or something. Anyway, Joe looked after it all.'

Noel thought. 'You're not Winston are you?'

Jaz grinned, not at all embarrassed. 'Sprung, mate,' he said. 'How did you know?'

'You're supposed to have a mohawk?'

'Yeah, well didn't want to look like a skinhead. Not when I heard about them bashing up poofs round the Coleherne. Shaved it off when I went to Brighton. New place, new start.'

Noel hunted for his wallet and took out his small photograph of Pomfrey. 'When you were at the sauna,' he said, 'did you see this man?'

Winston looked at the photo curiously. 'Not sure,' he said. 'Who is he?'

'He was my lover: Pomfrey Lister. I think he might have been at the Spartacus before he died.'

'Nah,' said Winston, thinking quickly. He liked Noel, but not enough to risk the problems identifying Pomfrey might create. 'My job was cleaning the place. Didn't really take much notice of the punters, matey.'

But there was sufficient hesitation for Noel to persist; he'd been undecided whether he wanted sex again with Jaz-Winston, but he needed to find out more. He put his hand on Jaz-Winston's shoulders and urged him towards the tube station: 'We can take the Northern line,' he said. 'My place isn't that far from the Angel. But what do I call you?'

'Guess I'm still Winston. At least in London.'

'And Jaz in the country,' said Noel, but the literary allusion was lost on Winston.

15

Arabella enjoyed hosting dinner parties, especially once she found a discreet Croatian caterer who would manage everything while making it appear that Arabella had spent the day cooking. Apart from Mary and Elvira they had invited a recently retired Vice Chancellor and her husband, a Tory backbencher who had surprisingly progressive views on relaxing drug laws and predictable prejudices on everything else. The six of them gathered in the front room for pre-dinner drinks and introductions.

'Sorry for your loss,' said the Vice Chancellor, meeting Mary for the first time. 'Your husband was a very significant researcher.'

Her husband nodded. 'I met him once,' he said. 'Chaired a panel he was on. Had to put him right on a couple of facts, though.' He chuckled. 'And ambitious. Get in a revolving door ahead of him and he'd still manage to come out in front.'

Mary remembered both the MP and the panel, a discussion on how to support British biomedical research. As she recalled, the chair had made several inaccurate assertions and looked very pleased with himself as he did so. Her hands tightened around her wine glass, resisting the urge to throw the contents at the man's face. His wife sensed her discomfort. 'Brilliant man,' said the Vice Chancellor hurriedly. 'And you yourself work in this field I believe?'

'I do,' said Mary. 'Our work has saved many young women from infection and premature death. I believe it is crucial to give young women the moral fibre to stand up for decency.'

'Indeed,' said Spencer. 'Mary's organisation has done sterling work with women and young girls ...' He turned to Elvira. 'I hope the Trust might cooperate even more fully with Mary's NGO now.'

Elvira looked slightly uneasy, but before she could reply Arabella announced that they should move into the dining room. This was a large rectangular room overlooking a quiet back lane, with a high stone wall against which climbed a profusion of red, lavender and white sweet peas. The room was dominated by a solid oak dining table, covered with a fine lace tablecloth and lit by a crystal chandelier. Along one wall was a long sideboard, in the centre of which was a large vase of white chrysanthemums.

Arabella carefully steered the conversation away from Pomfrey and the future of the Trust, asking how many of them had been to any of the shows currently on offer in the West End. It was a season of musical revivals, but other than her no-one seemed very interested in revisiting *Calamity Jane* or *Joseph and the Amazing Technicolor Dreamcoat*. Elvira said that she'd planned to visit the Globe Theatre before returning to Norway, and the Vice Chancellor spoke warmly of a production of *Streetcar Named Desire* in which a former student had been an understudy. 'I taught English,' she said complacently. 'Before I moved into management. I still kept my hand in, gave a few lectures to the undergrads.'

From theatre Arabella steered them onto politics, asking the Tory MP whether he saw anything positive about the current government. Despite warning looks from his wife he launched into a long litany of government failures, luckily interrupted by the arrival of the main course, an elaborate platter of roast lamb surrounded by walnuts and figs, served with roast potatoes and Jerusalem artichokes. This led to a long discussion about what exactly is a Jerusalem artichoke, with some agreement that it was neither from Jerusalem nor an artichoke.

As the dinner plates were being cleared away by the discrete

Croatian helper there was an awkward pause. Elvira turned to Mary.

'Mary, does the term Righteous mean anything to you?'

Mary gulped and Spencer, at the other end of the table, looked alarmed.

'Well,' she said slowly, 'we do speak of the Lord as righteous. Is that what you have in mind?'

'Could there be someone calling themself Righteous whom you've come across?'

Mary shook her head slowly, looking at Spencer for support. 'We come across so many people in our line of work,' he said soothingly. 'Maybe it's a group we're not aware of.'

He turned the conversation towards the Vice Chancellor. 'Perhaps,' he said, 'you might fill us in on some of the exciting projects you've been working on?'

Dessert followed—a baba au rhum with strawberries—and they returned to the morning room for coffee and liqueurs. Mary claimed a headache and left early, with many wishes of commiseration. She drove across the city, skirting the new traffic exclusion zone and curving past Hyde and Regent's Parks, then through the Heath. Normally she enjoyed the night drive through London, but now she was oblivious of her surroundings. How much, she wondered, did Elvira know?

That night she couldn't sleep. She roamed about the house, sensing Pomfrey's presence even more than when he'd been alive. The two abstract paintings in the living room, in particular, had been his choice, mementoes of his time as a graduate student in Baltimore, and she decided they should be auctioned. She would replace them with good reproductions of some of her favourite Impressionist paintings—and maybe she should totally refurbish his study, turn it into a proper guest room for people who might be visiting from her charity. Yes, she should get rid of everything that was too reminiscent of Pomfrey, even perhaps the photographs— but when she looked at the few photographs of them together, younger, more innocent, she was seized with an urge to cry and went into the kitchen in search of comfort food. The early hours of the morning found her curled up in front of the television set, eating a now cold custard pie, and watching programs of which she would have no memory.

∞

Winston left Noel's place in the early evening to visit his mother. They had spent a few hours together, mainly talking; the sex, they agreed, was fun, possibly to be repeated. Noel made them ham sandwiches and talked a lot about his relations with Pomfrey. Winston was a sympathetic listener, even though he denied any romantic experiences of his own. 'Lots of sex, matey,' he said, 'sometimes for fun, sometimes for cash. But I don't go for this soppy love stuff.'

After he came back from Brighton, Noel had hunted for newspaper photos of Pomfrey, and he took them out to show to Winston, who claimed he didn't recognise him. Pomfrey might have been at the Spartacus that evening, he agreed, but he'd been busy cleaning rooms, it was a full night with the leather crowd, and he had noticed several patrons who wandered around dressed in leather and rubber despite the heat of the sauna. What he didn't tell Noel was his own growing suspicion that the body he'd found was Pomfrey, and that Joe had recognised him. He thought he should tell Noel, but was uneasy about what Joe might do if he did; on the tube and bus to Stoke Newington he puzzled away at the dilemma and resolved to call Noel before he went back to Brighton.

The call came Monday morning when Noel had gone into the shop to unpack a new consignment of books, including some lesser-known works of Patricia Highsmith, and rearrange the shelves. As soon he was off the phone from Winston he called Sylvie, who was in the Trust offices working methodically through the backlog of messages and invoices from the Conference.

'Can we catch up?' he asked, 'I've got news—I can't tell you on the phone—it's serious though.' His voice broke, 'I was right:

Pomfrey *was* in the sauna that night. He *died* there.'

'No,' said Sylvie, 'he died at home. Mary told me—'

'She was lying. Please, I need to talk with you about it.'

Sylvie thought. 'OK,' she said, 'I can finish up early. Can you come to the café on the corner near my offices?'

The afternoon passed agonisingly slowly; Noel arrived at the café twenty minutes early, to make sure he could find a quiet outside table. As soon as Sylvie arrived he grabbed her and almost pushed her onto a seat.

'He told me,' said Noel, struggling to make sense of the short conversation with a reluctant Winston. 'He found him in a cubicle at the sauna. Dead.'

'Slow down,' said Sylvie. 'Let me get you a drink.' She went inside, ordered two beers, and returned. 'Now,' she said, 'who found him?'

In fits and starts Noel recounted the whole story of meeting Jaz—who was really Winston—of spending time with him, of the nervous phone call in which Winston acknowledged he had found a dead body in a cubicle, and who, though he couldn't be certain, was probably Pomfrey.

'But that doesn't make sense,' said Sylvie. 'There must have been a death certificate and that would have shown that he died at home. Unless—'

'I've thought and thought,' said Noel. 'Someone must have taken the body back to his house. And maybe Mary found him in bed and assumed he'd died there. Can you ask her?'

'She's asked me to come over tomorrow,' said Sylvie. 'She sounded pretty exhausted.'

16

Mary's living room seemed less immaculate than usual. The lilacs that had been so fresh last time were drooping, obviously long past their time, and there was a stain, probably from wine, on the coffee table. Mary herself was puffy-eyed and her hair was unusually unkempt. It was five o'clock; 'Thankfully,' said Mary, walking over to the well-stocked art deco drinks cabinet, 'we can have a G & T.'

Sylvie sank into one of the comfortable armchairs in the room, not sure why Mary had summoned her. She was nervous about raising Pomfrey's death, but Mary wanted to talk.

'I don't know whom else I can talk to,' she said, leaning forward anxiously. 'I feel I need to tell someone—' She stopped abruptly, took a swig from her glass. 'I think—cone of silence, please—what if I told you I think Pomfrey was going to leave me?'

Sylvie sensed she was on the verge of tears and said nothing.

'I think there may have been someone else—that's happened before, though it's never been serious. Pomfrey wasn't all that interested in sex—at least not with me. But this time—we'd had a fight. He hated what my organisation was doing in Uganda. I feel so guilty that was the last time we talked.'

'Mary,' said Sylvie tentatively, 'did Pomfrey really die at home?'

Mary blanched, looked away. 'Whatever gave you that idea?' she asked.

'Someone told Noel—'

'Noel? Who's Noel?' Mary almost shrieked, clutching her glass so hard it threatened to shatter.

Shit, thought Sylvie. She didn't know.

'I think,' said Sylvie carefully, 'he was a friend of Pomfrey's. And maybe he heard from a friend of his ...' She stopped, not sure how much she should say.

Mary blew her nose hard, holding back tears. 'It was so humiliating,' she said. 'It would have undermined all the important work I'm trying to do. I couldn't have people know Pomfrey was ... what has this Noel person told you? Who is he?'

'Mary,' said Sylvie, 'was Pomfrey's body brought here the night he died? Do you know where he'd been?'

Mary shuddered, remembering the night. 'Yes,' she said, almost whispering, 'he'd been in a men's club—a homosexual men's club. Of course,' she added, though without much conviction, 'he mightn't have known. He might just have wanted to go for a steam and a sauna. But the scandal if it had come out—Spencer helped me, he arranged to bring the body back home.'

'And you asked Alejandro to provide the death certificate?'

'We thought it better to ask someone who would be loyal. Alejandro was a close colleague; we knew he would be discreet.' Mary straightened her back, seeking to regain control. 'After all, he was dead. It was better for everyone if he had died here, peacefully.'

Sylvie nodded, unwilling to pursue the matter further. The conversation moved on uneasily to safer topics, but as soon as Sylvie left Mary rushed to telephone Spencer. Elvira's mention of Righteous and the fact that Sylvie seemed to know that Pomfrey had died in the sauna was making her increasingly nervous.

'We're fine,' said Spencer reassuringly. After Mary's call he had driven immediately to Highgate, concerned that she might call someone else. 'So who's the person who knows that Pomfrey was found dead in the Spartacus sauna?'

'Someone called Noel,' said Mary. 'But Sylvie didn't tell me anything about him. Or how he knew Pomfrey.' She looked away.

'Do you think—could Pomfrey have been interested in men?'

Spencer seemed taken aback by the question. 'Well,' he said, 'he did come across a lot of homosexuals in his research. And he and Alejandro had a research project that involved that place. He was probably there to check up how it was going.'

But even as he said it he had a vivid memory of Pomfrey's naked body in the cubicle, surely not a likely position for any researcher, however diligent.

'So far,' said Spencer, thinking aloud, 'the only people who know what happened are us and Joe, from the sauna. And Alejandro: do you know where he was that evening, when you called him? Doesn't he live somewhere in Berkshire?'

'He wasn't at home,' said Mary. 'I paged him, and he called me back on his Blackberry. He said something about being in town to check up on one of his research projects.'

Spencer thought. 'This chap—Noel?' he asked. 'Do you know who he is?'

Mary shook her head. 'Friend of Sylvie's I think. But how he knew Pomfrey ...' her voice trailed off as she contemplated the possibilities.

'I just wanted everything to go away,' she said. 'That's why I wanted him cremated as soon as possible. In case anyone started asking—if they knew he'd died in—that place—there would have had to be an autopsy.'

Driving back home through the slow twilight Spencer decided that Mary had become too unreliable to become Trust chair. If he were to block Alejandro he needed another alternative. He would need to placate Mary, maybe offer to help raise funds for her charity, while keeping it at arm's length.

After Spencer left, Mary went upstairs to Pomfrey's study. She had barely entered it since his death and it remained as he had left it, an open computer on the large wooden desk which overlooked the garden, papers stacked high on a small side table which still held a half-drunk glass of sparkling water. A dying fly buzzed nosily against the window and an empty ashtray, souvenired many years ago from a hotel in Lausanne, still sat on top of the desk. Mary glanced at the table, then opened the top drawer of the desk, looking for an address book. The drawer was surprisingly full—Pomfrey had apparently not thrown away old credit card and bank statements—but the address book was easily found, a small book bound in dark green vellum in which she had seen Pomfrey jot down entries. Most of the names seemed many years old, some of them fading with time, but it was easy enough to find Noel: no surname, just a telephone number. On a whim Mary dialled the number; there was a recorded message saying: *The shop is unattended, please try us later.*

She rang back several times the next morning before the shop opened, and hung up when Noel answered, but not before catching the name of the shop. Camden Town was close; she decided to check it out. Forty minutes later she was standing outside *Mackie's Loved Used Books*, trying to appear casual as she peered in, looking for someone who might be Noel.

At the back of the shop, where a small counter nestled between several bookstacks, she could make out a thin young man with longish brown hair, but his face was obscured; she could go in and ask—no, she was too nervous—she walked away, trying to compose her thoughts. Uncertain she walked round the block, and when she came back Noel was stooped over a pile of books in the front of the shop, and she was scared he might notice her. She turned away, but she knew, suddenly and definitely, that this was the person for whom Pomfrey had been planning to leave her. She clenched her fists hard, trying to regain composure, and felt a surge of pure hatred for Noel, for what he represented, for those few moments when Pomfrey had tried to talk to her about his desires and she had cut him off, refused to accept that he was other than a middle-aged man with declining libido. If she were honest with herself, had her own developing dislike of homosexuals been linked to her growing suspicions about Pomfrey?

ᙣ

That evening Spencer paid a call on Joe, making sure he could enter the sauna through the back entrance. He was becoming more uneasy about the Trust's investments in Spartacus and hoped to back out, but Joe was adamant that this would be difficult. 'Not that easy, mate,' he said. 'The money's tied up in renovations, not as if it were sitting there waiting for you to treat Spartacus like a cash machine.'

'It would be bad for us all,' said Spencer, 'if anyone connected Pomfrey with this place. Might lead to too many questions being asked.'

'Right,' said Joe. 'So we all keep our mouths shut. Who knows anyway?'

'Mary mentioned someone called Noel—do you know who he is?'

Joe shook his head, but of course he did. The young bloke who'd accosted him in Brighton, and who seemed to be on the prowl. It was time, thought Joe, to do a little hunting himself. Rahid, he knew, was on duty the following evening, and he might know something.

17

Winston took the morning train back to Brighton with a backpack of clothes he'd left at his mother's. Unpacking it he found an old hoodie that he'd worn on his last day working at Spartacus; in one of the pockets was a small empty vial, labelled insulin. He was sure it was something he'd picked up off the floor after he returned to Pomfrey's cubicle with Joe, and that it had not been there forty minutes earlier when he'd cleaned out the cubicle for the first time that evening. He had already been uneasy with Noel's assurance that Pomfrey had died from a sudden heart attack. Maybe the empty insulin vial would help explain what happened?

His first instinct was to forget about it, but Winston had a strong sense of duty. He wondered whether he might ask Joe if it meant anything, but he was a little frightened of antagonising Joe. Perhaps, he thought, he could look for Rahid, whom he'd always liked, and ask his advice. He'd agreed to come back to London later that week to take his mother to the optometrist. And he remembered that Rahid was rostered to do massage on Wednesday evenings; even if he'd best not enter the sauna he had a fair idea when Rahid would have signed off for the night, and he could wait for him outside.

Wednesday evening found him loitering on the footpath near enough to the Spartacus entrance to see anyone who came out without it being too obvious that he was waiting. It was the last moments of twilight and there was a slight haze in the air, which was turning chilly. Winston snuggled into his hoodie, which he'd worn constantly since retrieving it, and paced along the street, quiet except for a distant car alarm which seemed to start and stop spasmodically. Two men came out of the sauna, their arms touching, and as they walked past him they paused for a moment. 'Raf,' said one of the men; 'Anthony,' replied the other. 'It's 18 Clifton Street, don't forget'.

Winston checked his watch again. It was already past the time Rahid should have finished, when he saw him come out of the sauna and turn to walk in the opposite direction.

'Hey!' Winston ran after him. Rahid swung round. 'Winston,' he said, 'what the fuck—?'

'Can I talk to you? Can we go somewhere?'

Rahid hesitated. 'Sure,' he said, 'let's get a drink.'

There was a small pub on a nearby corner, a grimy grey brick building that had had stood firm against rapid gentrification, bare plaster walls with a couple of tattered portraits of the Queen above the bar, reminders of last year's Jubilee. A small group of men clustered in front of a TV set in the front bar, but they took their beers through to a small backyard where they were alone, except for a white-haired woman who sat chain smoking by the back fence.

'So,' said Rahid, 'what's up?'

'The night Pomfrey Lister died,' began Winston, 'you were in the sauna, right?'

'I'd left,' said Rahid firmly. 'I know nothing about it.'

Winston explained: how he'd met Noel in Brighton, how after talking with Noel he'd identified Pomfrey as the man whose body he'd discovered in the sauna that evening, Joe's eagerness to get rid of him, his growing sense that there was something wrong with the official version of how Pomfrey had died, and his discovery of the insulin.

'But,' said Rahid, 'that bottle might have been there for days.'

'No,' said Winston. 'I cleaned out the cubicle less than an hour earlier. I remember, because someone had spilt amyl and I scrubbed the floor. There was nothing there.'

'Maybe he was a diabetic,' said Rahid. 'Don't diabetics have to inject themselves regularly?'

'He died from a heart attack, right? Could insulin bring one on?'

'It could,' said Rahid. 'But like I said, I wasn't there.'

'So how did the body get from Spartacus to his house?'

Rahid shrugged. 'As I said, mate, I wasn't there. I'd stop listening to this guy, Noel. Sounds to me as if he's got a chip on his shoulder.' He stood up. 'Winston,' he said firmly, 'the man's dead. No point asking awkward questions about him now. If your mate's got some real evidence why doesn't he go to the police?'

☙

Elvira had not become a leading epidemiologist without a certain dogged determination. She had fond memories of working with Pomfrey when he established the Trust, and she felt an obligation to find out more before she was willing to decide whom she would support to replace him. She had noted Mary's shock at the mention of Righteous, and she recalled Pomfrey's insistence that the Trust stay at arm's length from Mary's organisation.

Six months earlier she had invited Pomfrey to Oslo to deliver a lecture, and they dined afterwards on top of one of the city's modern hotels, overlooking the harbour. It had been an early winter's evening, when the air was crisp and dark, with a view across the railway station to the Opera House, its white fins stretching out towards the water, ferry lights tracing flimsy skeins towards the southern shores of the fjord. Pomfrey had been eloquent on the need to reach out to marginalised populations in the fight against HIV, and the ways in which some organisations working in the field were preventing clear messages. 'People have sex,' he said. 'They shoot up. They do things governments like to pretend don't happen. We have to acknowledge that.' He had not mentioned Mary by name, but when Elvira asked him about her work with *God Loves Us All* he had looked angry and quickly changed the subject.

On a hunch Elvira contacted an old friend who was an anthropologist in one of London's Universities and whom she knew had collaborated with several projects funded by the Trust in East Africa. Her friend was travelling, but through email Elvira learnt that Pomfrey had questioned her about a program for 'converting' lesbians and gay men, in part funded by American fundamentalists, in East Africa. Asked whether she knew if the program might be called Righteous her friend sent back a one-word answer in capitals: YES. Elvira closed her computer and decided it was time to talk with Alejandro.

He replied to her message instantly and suggested a meeting on Southbank near her hotel. 'I'll meet you at the café on Gabriel's Wharf,' he said. 'We can speak privately there.'

Elvira arrived early and walked down to the small sandy strip that clung to the bank of the Thames. It was deserted, but for a couple of children throwing beachballs back and forth, and a solitary sunbaker, stretched out on the grainy sand, ignoring the breeze that swept off the river. She walked past several shops selling the sort of expensive objects tourists might buy and regret once they got home, then settled down to wait for Alejandro. He arrived slightly out of breath, tense, clearly eager to make the right impression.

'So sad,' he said, 'Pomfrey's death. And so pleased you are here trying to sort things out.'

Elvira nodded.

'The Trust,' he said earnestly, 'needs strong leadership. We all admired Pomfrey, of course, and his vision in setting up the Trust. But recently—how can I put it?—his grasp of the research data was a little slapdash.'

Elvira raised her eyebrows, still saying nothing.

'An important researcher, his work around hepatitis was groundbreaking,' said Alejandro carefully. 'But frankly he was becoming an obstacle in the vaccine work. I hate to say it, but we're better off without him.'

'You had disagreements?'

'I was convinced we were ready to proceed to human trials. He opposed my approach, but that was because he was determined that the vaccine be *his* discovery. He could be ruthless—look at the way he controlled the Trust.'

'Isn't Spencer the person who basically runs the Trust?'

Alejandro snorted. 'He certainly likes to give that impression. I'd believe him even less than I'd believed Pomfrey. The two of them kept everyone else in the dark, especially where money was concerned. Now that Pomfrey's gone we need to open it up, get rid of Spencer.'

'What do you mean, where money is concerned?'

'I've no actual proof. But I suspect they were using Trust finances in some bad investments. I overheard a conversation; Pomfrey seemed angry about some misuse of Trust funds.'

'Did Pomfrey ever say anything about that to you?'

'Of course not. Pomfrey was always clear who ruled the roost. In the labs and at the Trust.'

He sounded bitter and Elvira changed the subject. 'Does the term Righteous mean anything to you?' she asked.

Alejandro shook his head. 'It's a religious reference?'

'I think someone—or some group—was trying to interfere with our work in reaching vulnerable communities. Especially men who have sex with men.'

'Well,' said Alejandro meaningfully, 'that would not have been Pomfrey. He took a very strong—a personal—interest in homosexuals.' He lowered his voice. 'We had a project working with a gay venue, a spa and sauna in Shoreditch. I think Pomfrey visited there more often than he needed, if you catch my meaning.'

'He told you?'

'I saw him,' said Alejandro, 'the night he died—' He stopped, conscious that he'd said more than was wise. 'That is, I overheard him telling someone that he needed to go to the Spartacus to check on some drugs ... Those places,' he added, in a sudden burst of repressed anger, 'trade in drugs.'

'You're surely not suggesting that Pomfrey died from a drug overdose?'

'No,' said Alejandro firmly, 'he had some underlying health issues—Mary was clear about that. And, of course, he died at home.'

He looked at Elvira, unsure whether he could trust her, but he needed to vent. So called recreational drugs were exploding across various subcultures, leading to dependency, psychosis, even suicides. The people who provided the drugs were criminals, but very rarely caught and prosecuted.

'I am sure,' said Alejandro, 'that the Spartacus is a conduit for ecstasy and opioids, and maybe Pomfrey knew but was unwilling to act because he was a client and didn't want that known.'

'Have you talked to the sauna directly?' asked Elvira. 'Maybe you could warn them?'

Alejandro shrugged, but he knew she was right. Much as he disliked it he needed to return to the sauna and find the manager.

☙

Rahid was towelling down his last client for the evening, a slightly corpulent businessman who liked to have his feet tickled and who tipped well, when Joe sent a message asking him to come down to the office. Rahid stretched, flexed his shoulders and went to the back stairs that led to the office, windowless and humid from the adjoining laundry.

'This bugger Noel,' said Joe. 'What do you know about him?'

Rahid hesitated. 'Not much,' he said, wondering whether he would get away with total denial. 'Only that he was a friend—maybe more than a friend—of Prof. Lister.'

'So why is he asking so many questions? What does he know?'

Rahid shrugged. 'He's been asking around. I don't think he knows anything.'

'You know,' said Joe deliberately, 'that Lister died here. Sudden heart attack, his wife insisted we take the body to her place. That is *not* to be repeated mate.'

Rahid nodded.

'Only people who know are me, Lister's wife, Spencer Carson, that bloke Professor Herrera who did the death certificate—you know him?'

'Sure,' said Rahid, 'professionally. He runs that research project here on sexual behaviours. I think he was in the sauna that evening. Earlier, before I left.' He looked at Joe. 'Why have you told me?'

'You'll keep your mouth shut,' said Joe, winking. 'I've told you because I think you know more than you're letting on.'

Rahid stayed silent.

'And,' added Joe, 'you might be able to help me find that bloke Noel. Do you know where he is? Might need to have a few words.'

'No,' said Rahid, 'but I might be able to find out.'

'You think Lister's wife would know?'

'Unlikely,' said Rahid. 'I think whatever else he was Prof. was very closeted. She would have gone spare if she'd known about him.'

CB

But Mary not only knew where to find Noel, she was beginning to follow him. At first it was only quick glances through the shop window, then a day or so later she went into the shop, thought of engaging him in conversation when she was pre-empted by a customer, who was determined to find an original edition of Gibbons' *Decline and Fall of the Roman Empire* and refused to accept Noel's response that it was a three-volume set worth many tens of thousands. Timidly Mary withdrew

The following evening she was outside the shop at closing time and managed to get a clear view of Noel. He had a weak chin, she thought, but she was struck by his eyes, surprisingly black given his otherwise pale colouring. She watched as he pulled down the shutters and locked the front door, but he clearly left the shop from the rear and she was too embarrassed to follow him.

Noel was too agitated to go home after Sylvie had called to tell him about her conversation with Mary, and too restless to go to a bar or café. He wandered towards Kings Cross, passing the mottled drab brick of St Pancras Hospital, vaguely aware that it had once been a workhouse and infirmary. He crossed into Bloomsbury and decided to drop in at *Gay's the Word* and browse their new books. But the shop was crowded for a reading by a visiting Australian, whose book *The Prosperous Thief* was on display in the windows, and he walked on. He thought that he could walk the whole night across London without seeing anyone he knew, and he felt desperately alone. Oddly the one person he most wanted to see was Winston, but he was presumably back in Brighton, working in whichever of Joe's businesses he was managing, and Noel had only a scrawled phone number which he had left in the shop.

This is when I should go to the gym, thought Noel, but he had not succumbed to the gay imperative to sculpt his body; exercise for Noel was long solitary walks, and almost automatically he headed towards Soho. At Tottenham Court he had a sudden urge to take the tube and return to the Spartacus, but that was a bad idea, maybe he could find quick sex on the street and temporarily kill his anxiety. But the groups of men outside the bars seemed younger, buffer, more confident, and Noel felt intimidated. He walked over to Soho Square and found an empty bench. It was twilight and people were packing up their picnic belongings, leaving a few teenagers to play desultory table tennis in one corner.

A middle-aged woman carrying a large shopping bag sat down beside him and smiled at him. 'You look lost' she said softly. She took out a packet of shortbread from her bag and offered him a piece. 'For the birds,' she said, scattering more pieces around the bench.

'Not really lost,' said Noel. 'Just not sure how to move on.'

'Oh, my dear,' said the woman earnestly, 'that's what life is. A constant circle of hellos and goodbyes. Knowing which is which is what matters.'

Noel nodded, not sure whether this was profound or just silly. The woman fished in her bag again and took out a packet of cigarettes and some Nicorette gum. 'You see,' she said, 'it's a choice. What gives us pleasure isn't always good for us.' She sighed again, carefully replaced the gum and lit a cigarette. 'But doing what's sensible isn't always the best choice. Do what your gut tells you, even if it seems ridiculous.'

'Yes,' said Noel, standing. 'Thank you. Maybe I'll do just that.'

He would walk home via the shop he thought, call Winston and maybe arrange another trip to Brighton.

18

Spencer paced around his office, thinking how best to control the situation. He was less troubled by the contradiction between his investment in a gay sex venue and his support of homophobic programs in East Africa than he was by the potential scandal if it became known that he had diverted Trust resources to both. Pomfrey, he knew, had had suspicions. But now that Pomfrey was dead, maybe the blame could be placed on him. He rang Elvira and arranged a quiet dinner the following evening.

They met in a small Hungarian restaurant in Soho, a narrow room with white, green and red wallpaper and flowery tablecloths, which Elvira observed could serve as a dirndl skirt. But, she agreed, the food was excellent, and Spencer ordered the second most expensive Villany wine.

'I'd hoped to keep this quiet,' said Spencer unctuously, 'for Mary's sake. But I think you and the other Trustees need to know. Before he died Pomfrey had made some rather injudicious choices about Trust resources. Not ones he always chose to run past me.'

Elvira said nothing but sipped her wine appreciatively.

'I suspect he was diverting funds to his wife's charity,' said Spencer. 'The reference to Righteous—you know what that is?'

'I do now,' said Elvira. 'A program to "convert" young homosexual teenagers. Driven by hatred and poor science.'

'Yes. I'm sure Pomfrey didn't really approve of it,' replied Spencer, but with his wife involved he might have felt he had no choice.'

'Mary claims they argued about it.'

Spencer nodded, hoping he could persuade Mary to keep his own involvement hidden. 'That's not all,' he said, pausing while they ordered cherry strudel. 'I think Pomfrey might have diverted Trust funds into a gay sex venue. There's a sauna that homosexuals frequent, somewhere in Shoreditch, he knew the place through a research project. Maybe he thought this was a way of expatiating his guilt.'

Elvira nodded. 'I assume,' she said, 'that you have some evidence of this? The transfer of funds can't happen without authorisation.'

'Of course,' said Spencer. 'But you understand that the Trust was established with some unusual provisions. Only the chair or the chief executive officer—that's me—can authorise payments. We're meant to check on each other, but in the excitement of organising the Conference that might have been overlooked.'

'As trustees,' said Elvira carefully, 'don't we need to see a full record of financial dealings?'

'Of course, of course.' He nodded to the waiter to refill their glasses and leant towards her. 'But we have had several large bequests which were anonymous and came with restrictions on who could know about them. And we needed to invest some of our reserves to provide an ongoing income for the Trust.'

'The other trustees have asked me to get a clear statement of the financial position. Once we have that we can proceed to replace Pomfrey.'

'And you might be interested ...?'

Elvira smiled. 'I wondered whether you might ask me that,' she said.

ෆ

Alejandro parked his car a block away and walked towards the entrance of the sauna. He had to stand behind several men who were checking in, and he was relieved that none of them even glanced at him.

'And you are?' asked Paolo, back on reception. He winked when Alejandro pointed to the flyer promoting their sexual behaviour research study and called out to Joe, who was filling in at the drinks counter.

'Can we talk somewhere private?' asked Alejandro.

Joe nodded and took him back to his office. There was just room for Joe's desk, a couple of rickety chairs and an old steel filing cabinet on which sat a couple of family photographs.

'I assume,' said Alejandro officiously, 'that our survey will continue despite Pomfrey's unfortunate death?'

Joe nodded.

'But that's not why I'm here today.'

He paused, looking hard at Joe.

'My son,' said Alejandro, who had rehearsed his approach, 'is in a rehab facility only a few blocks away. His life has been ruined by drugs.'

Joe looked at him impassively. 'Sorry to hear that, mate.'

'If you're supplying kids like Carlos you are destroying their lives. I think Spartacus is supplying amphetamines.'

'Your mate Lister thought that too. Either of you got any proof?' Joe stood up, emphasising his size. 'Look,' he said, 'I can't control everything that goes on here. But you want to be careful making accusations.'

'We could work together,' said Alejandro. 'Try to stop this infernal trade.'

'Or else?' Joe cracked his knuckles. 'Seems to me you're hardly in a position to make demands. You knew perfectly well that Lister died here, and we took the body back to his house. You signed the certificate, mate. That could be a case of malpractice if it got out.'

'I examined the body. It was heart failure.'

'Sure,' said Joe. 'But what caused the failure?'

He leant over, his face almost touching Alejandro. 'See, mate, I know you were here that evening. Maybe you even did the geezer in.'

'That's ridiculous!' Now Alejandro stood, at least a head shorter than Joe. 'If anything like that happened you were the one with the motive. Pomfrey was onto you. Maybe we should just take it to the police—or do you have a guilty conscience?'

Joe grinned. 'Relax mate,' he said, 'we're both sweet. Leave it be. And if it makes you happy I'll check into whether any of my blokes are selling stuff they shouldn't.'

Joe put his arm around Alejandro and ushered him out.

'Take care,' he said, 'I'd hate you to have an accident, mate.'

Joe was confident Alejandro could be managed. He was more concerned about Noel, but he had a hunch that Rahid would find him.

∞

Caitlin was proud of her basement flat. It sat beneath a white terrace house in Bayswater, three rooms opening out onto a small courtyard. There was little natural light but she had created an impression of space with several strategically placed mirrors and a pair of standard lamps, lovingly rescued from junk shops. There was a large open living area, giving onto her much smaller bedroom, and the walls were covered with framed posters marking the politics of the past century, including a large image of a woman standing triumphant on the ruins of the Berlin Wall.

When Sylvie suggested they catch up Caitlin had invited her to dinner and spontaneously told Rahid to join them. He might, she thought, be able to tell them more about Pomfrey's last evening at the sauna. Had he known Sylvie would be there Rahid would not have agreed, but he and Sylvie arrived at the same moment and after the flurry of greetings it was too difficult to extricate himself.

'Of course,' said Caitlin, 'you know each other. You both worked with Prof. Lister.'

Rahid nodded. 'He was my supervisor.' He looked at Sylvie, unsure what she might know. 'We didn't always get on, but he was a top man in the field.'

Caitlin interrupted with offers of drinks and homemade pasta, leading them to the small dining alcove where she had laid out plates. The pasta was delicious—fettucine alfredo with mushrooms—and Caitlin guided the conversation to a general roundup of politics in which they could agree to deplore the latest news from Iraq and the perfidy of the Blair government. The fettucine finished they moved back to the living area for coffee and biscuits.

'Caitlin and I have been playing tennis,' said Sylvie, falling onto the sofa and kicking off her shoes. 'You should join us.'

'Nah,' said Rahid. 'I hate competitive sports.'

'It's interesting what one learns about people from watching how they play tennis,' said Caitlin. 'I've only seen you on the courts once,' she said, turning to Sylvie, 'but you seem to play methodically, calmly. It's not great tennis, but it keeps the ball in play long enough for the other side to make a mistake. The men usually like to show off, which means they are likely to go for big serves and miss half the time.'

Sylvie looked at her. 'Is that how Alejandro plays?' she asked.

'Absolutely. He's determined to win, and he likes to hit forehand drives to the back corner. And he can get very angry if they go out. I've seen him almost come to blows over a line call.'

Rahid nodded. 'He can be very determined,' he said. 'That's not always a bad thing.'

'You know he was the person who certified Pomfrey's death,' said Sylvie. 'Which as it turns out might not have happened at home.'

She looked at Rahid, wondering how much he knew.

'Have you found out something?' asked Rahid.

'Mary admits he died at the Spartacus sauna and the body was taken back to the house. That's where you work, isn't it Rahid?'

'Sure. But I wasn't there. Guess he collapsed with a heart attack and Joe moved the body.'

'Are we sure it was a heart attack?' asked Caitlin, sensing his unease. 'What if it was something else?'

'Like what?' Rahid grinned. 'You suggesting the old guy was bumped off?'

The two women looked at him, not sure if he was joking. 'I mean,' said Rahid, 'moving a body is not that easy. If you're right, there must have been a pretty good reason.'

'Mary said that the body was brought over by two men,' said Sylvie. 'Spencer and the sauna owner, Joe I think.'

Rahid nodded. 'And Professor Herrera?'

'No, he came later, to write the death certificate.'

Possibly, thought Rahid. But he knew Alejandro had been in the sauna that evening, and he was still thinking how best to make use of that knowledge.

'Something puzzles me,' said Sylvie. 'Mary was adamant that Pomfrey was diabetic, and that contributed to his heart problems. But I worked with him for three years, and there was no sign—I think he may even have discussed diabetes a couple of times, never any suggestion that he was speaking from his own experience.'

'But that's typical,' said Rahid. 'He was always very guarded about himself—no one in the labs ever knew much about the real Professor Lister.'

He stood up. 'Got to get going. Maybe you're asking too many questions. It could just get you into trouble.' He kissed Caitlin on the cheek and left.

The two women looked at each other: 'What have we got ourselves into?' said Sylvie anxiously. 'Maybe he's right, we should drop it.'

'No.' Caitlin leant towards her. 'We owe it to Pomfrey to find out what happened. You see that, don't you?'

Sylvie nodded. 'I've met Pomfrey's regular doctor,' she said. 'He came to the offices when Pomfrey had a reaction to a yellow fever inoculation. I think I might try to talk to him.'

19

Mary, once so organised, felt routine slipping from her. She was sleeping erratically, skipping meals or else binging on foods she would once have dismissed as unhealthy. One day she grabbed the vacuum cleaner and approached the carpets with the ferocity of a motor mower; other days she left dishes to pile up in the sink. She was obsessed with Noel, but unsure what she wanted from him. For a week or so she found excuses to go to Camden High Street, to walk past the bookshop as if to reassure herself that he was still there. Joe, who had discovered from Rahid where he might find Noel, had yet to decide how he wanted to approach him.

 C8

The day after his dinner with Caitlin and Sylvie, Rahid met Alejandro to discuss his thesis. He decided he would use the meeting to ask for a research position back in the labs. If he were associated with the discovery of an HIV vaccine his career would be assured, and he thought he could persuade Alejandro.

'I'm still puzzled about Professor Lister's death,' he said, after some discussion of his thesis findings, and how he might rewrite the synopsis. 'Now *I* had a good reason to be in the sauna that evening. But I'm not sure why you were there—'

'I was checking in on our survey,' said Alejandro firmly. 'As was my obligation.'

'And both you and Prof. Lister were there because of the survey?' Rahid's voice expressed some surprise. 'Wasn't that something you would delegate to one of your psychologist collaborators?'

'I didn't know Pomfrey was there—I didn't see him.'

'But you know he died there?'

'Rahid,' said Alejandro, 'I'm not sure what you are driving at.'

'Let's be honest, Prof. We both had reasons to dislike Pomfrey Lister.'

Alejandro stood up. 'This conversation is at an end,' he said. 'We will not discuss what happened that evening ever again if you want to work with me.'

Rahid nodded and stood up to leave. He wondered why Alejandro was so nervous and how he might best take advantage of that.

␣

Noel worked late that evening. Mrs Mackie had dropped by with a large carton of old paperbacks, mainly British war stories with lurid covers of planes and explosions, and he was sorting through them, looking for anything that might be of interest to their regular customers. He had talked with Winston, who was vague about his plans but thought he might be back in London that weekend, and he planned to leave the shop after seven, and get a meal at the local pub. Just as he was pulling down the shutters the phone rang, and a man asked if he were Noel. 'Right,' said the man, 'just checking,' and hung up. Puzzled Noel walked out onto the street.

A white delivery van sped past, and behind it Noel heard the sound of a car suddenly accelerating. The car was clearly driving too fast, he thought, when he realised it was heading towards him. It veered up onto the pavement. Had there not been a driveway to dive into it might well have hit him. There was a loud beep of the horn and the car sped off. Shaken, Noel slumped down on the footpath, wondering if someone had deliberately tried to hit him, and if so why. A passing cyclist stopped and helped him back on his feet.

'Wow, that was close, man. You okay?'

'I think so,' said Noel. 'I'll be fine.' His arm was slightly sore, and he started picking bits of gravel off his wrist, where he had broken his fall. The cyclist, reassured, rode off.

Noel retraced his steps back to the shop and slumped into the old chair behind the counter. Need to stay calm, he told himself, but what if it was deliberate? Was someone out to get him, and why? He rang Sylvie, hoping she might reassure him. She tried to dismiss it as no more than a car accidentally out of control, but she agreed to meet the following evening, this time at the First Out Cafe Bar near Tottenham Court, one of the few gay places in London where both Noel and Sylvie felt totally comfortable. The café was almost full with a range of people, heavily tattooed women sharing the space with a couple of drag queens and a small group of workmen in singlets and shorts.

'I'm sure it was an accident,' she said, after Noel recounted the incident. 'After all who would want to hurt you?'

'Maybe the same person who wanted to hurt Pomfrey? Sylvie, I've thought and thought. If he died in the sauna—and there were people so anxious to cover it up that they removed the body—that means someone was behind his death.'

Sylvie prodded her organic spinach salad reflectively. 'Yes, she said reluctantly, 'you might be right. I rang his GP, who was very non-committal. But he sounded surprised when I asked about diabetes. I don't know why Mary was so insistent.'

'Maybe she's trying to hide something? Perhaps she knows what happened at the sauna and she's covering up.' He squeezed his cup, as if it might give him the answer. 'Could it have been suicide?'

'No,' said Sylvie firmly. 'He would hardly have killed himself just before the Conference—that was going to be his great triumph. Rahid knows something, but he's not saying. He seems to think

Alejandro is involved.'

Noel looked puzzled. 'Didn't he sign the death certificate?'

'Exactly. He had quarrelled with Pomfrey a few days earlier. And apparently he was in the sauna that night.'

'And helped move the body?'

'I don't think so. That was Spencer and Joe—the sauna manager. Maybe your friend Winston knows more?'

'I'm not sure he's a friend yet. I like him, though.'

He looked at Sylvie. 'How are you doing?'

'I had a date last weekend,' said Sylvie, feeling the need to confide. 'Friend of my sister, an anaesthetist. Guess she thought we might have something in common, she's never understood that my work with Pomfrey was only administrative. He took me to a wine bar in Chelsea and talked non-stop about the financial crisis for their fucking football team and how it was going to be saved by some Russian oligarch. *And* his breath was bad.'

'So you won't be seeing him again, I assume?'

Sylvie sighed. 'I agreed to go to the theatre with him next week. But I suspect I'll have a migraine coming on and cancel.' She looked at him. 'Maybe you'll have better luck with Winston?'

'Not sure.' He sighed. 'I do miss Pomfrey,' he said. 'I felt safe with him, as if he would protect me whatever happened. I can't imagine Winston in that way.'

Winston had said to meet him at the George and Dragon late afternoon Saturday, before the pub got too crowded. It was close to Spartacus, and Winston knew a couple of the barmen. Inside the pub was stuffed with assorted cheap knickknacks and blown-up figures of gay icons, but beneath the camp fixtures was a solid British pub quite unlike the swishy Soho bars. In the background Bon Jovi was singing *All about lovin' you.*

'Hey,' said Winston, giving him a long, sloppy kiss. 'I've got something for you.'

He reached into his rather tattered backpack and took out the small vial of insulin he'd found in Pomfrey's cubicle the night of his death. 'This was lying next to the body,' he said. 'I picked it up automatically and then forgot about it. Not sure if it helps you at all?'

Noel read the instructions on the vial. 'Not sure,' he said, 'but I'll talk to Sylvie about it.'

'Don't tell anyone else, mate. I don't want Joe to know I found it and didn't tell him.'

'What about his glasses? Pomfrey would never have been far away from his glasses.'

'Not on him—and not in the cubicle. Pretty sure I'd have seen them.' Winston stroked Noel's arm. 'So, what are you drinking?'

He went to the bar, gave one of the barmen a high five, and returned with two beers. 'Guy at the bar's an American,' he said, 'from Tennessee. Hot sex if you're interested.'

Noel nodded, but his stomach knotted at what felt like a clear indication that Winston was no longer interested in him sexually. Winston sensed his reactions: 'Matey,' he said, 'we can still get it on together, just not tonight. Fuck around as much as you want—but safe.' He grinned. 'After the rumours that Freddy Mercury was positive I made every bloke I went with swear they only did safe sex.'

He hugged Noel. 'Mate,' he said, 'I need something rough and uncomplicated tonight. Why don't you come down to Brighton next weekend and hang out with me there?'

20

Sylvie was browsing the aisles of her local supermarket, fretting at the scarcity of choices for a single person, when she ran into the man she recognised as Pomfrey's doctor. They smiled tentatively as they both reached for a bottle of wine, then he asked her abruptly why she had rung him about Pomfrey's health.

'It was a shock,' said Dr. Cosby, 'I only heard after the cremation. I understand Mary called in someone else the night he died.'

'She said you were away.'

He shook his head. 'No,' he said, 'I was here—we live in Holloway, quite close. I'm over this side of town for a dinner party.' He examined the wine bottle reflectively, then replaced it. 'Why did you think Pomfrey was diabetic?'

'Mary told me—she thought that contributed to his heart attack.'

'No,' he said, 'no, he wasn't diabetic. After you rang I looked back at his last blood work. I have no idea why Mary thought that, but his sugar levels were totally normal. Nothing wrong with his heart either. Could I ask who examined him?'

'A colleague. One of the top HIV researchers.'

Dr. Cosby nodded. 'But of course,' he said thoughtfully, 'he wouldn't know anything of Pomfrey's medical history.'

'So he wouldn't be taking insulin?'

'Of course not. It's dangerous if not taken correctly.' The doctor looked at her curiously but then turned and walked off.

Sylvie mused on those words as she walked back to her flat. She remembered Rahid's offhand suggestion that maybe he'd been 'bumped off'—at the time she thought it was just bad taste, now she wasn't sure. The presence of the empty insulin vial needed to be investigated. She confided in Caitlin as they drove out to tennis the following afternoon.

'Do you think you should go to the police?' asked Caitlin, having heard about the doctor's comments and the insulin bottle.

'And say what?' said Sylvie. 'That I suspect Pomfrey was murdered—that someone injected him with insulin? But there's no body and he wasn't a diabetic? No, we need to find out more about what happened in the sauna that night, and who was there.'

'Rahid can help us,' said Caitlin.

'Maybe. But isn't he also a suspect?'

'Rahid? I know he hated Pomfrey, but after all he was the one who suggested murder.'

'Classic double bluff.' Sylvie laughed. 'Come on, Caitlin, you've read Agatha Christie. Don't you know that everyone is a suspect?'

'Rahid seemed to think it was Alejandro. Who else is there?'

'What about Noel?'

'No,' said Sylvie, 'he was the one who discovered that the body had been moved. But his friend Winston, the attendant at the sauna … isn't it often the person who finds the body who's the most likely suspect? After all, it's only his word that he found the empty insulin bottle there—he could have planted it himself. And there are the chaps who moved the body: there's the owner, Joe I think he's called, and Spencer, but why was Spencer called in? And who called him?'

'That's five,' said Caitlin. 'Alejandro, Rahid, Winston, Spencer and Joe.'

'Five we know about.' Sylvie sighed. 'There would have been other men in the sauna, any one of them could have done it,'

'OK,' said Caitlin, 'but it's more likely to be someone who was connected to Pomfrey in some way. Maybe Noel's friend can find out about their movements that night.'

They had arrived. Sylvie wondered what it would be like to see Alejandro, now he was a possible suspect in what she increasingly believed was murder. But he was already warming up and rushed off once his match was finished. And, she thought, what could she ask him; Sylvie quailed at the idea of confronting someone with the idea of murder.

'Means, motive, opportunity,' said Caitlin as they drove back. 'That's what we need to establish.'

'If it *is* murder,' Sylvie sighed. 'Maybe we're just being over dramatic about the whole thing. Isn't it most likely he had a heart attack and was taken home, just as Mary said?'

'Perhaps we should start by asking Mary exactly what she knows? She must have been given some explanation.'

'Yes,' said Sylvie, 'that makes sense. And maybe see if Noel can get more out of his friend Winston.'

ങ

Sylvie arranged to visit Mary the following evening. In the week since she'd seen her, Mary seemed to have lost weight and her hair was being to look frazzled.

'I've told you everything I know,' said Mary defiantly. 'I don't want to talk any more about that awful evening.'

'Did you ever wonder,' asked Sylvie tentatively, 'Whether there was something not natural about Pomfrey's death?'

Mary stared at her. 'What are you suggesting? Pomfrey died of a sudden heart attack—the doctor said so.'

'But the doctor—Alejandro—wasn't there. How could he be so certain? After all, he wasn't Pomfrey's regular doctor.'

Mary, she noticed, was wringing her hands as if trying to keep control. 'Pomfrey had health issues,' she said firmly. 'He wasn't altogether satisfied with his regular doctor.'

'Did Alejandro help bring the body here?'

'No, that was Spencer and Joe, the manager I think he is. He'd rung Spencer and Spencer rang me—they knew each other through some AIDS program. Spencer was very helpful in working out what to do.' Mary stood up. 'I bought a quiche,' she said. 'Let me heat it up. But please—these suggestions are very hurtful. I think you've been reading too many bad mystery stories.'

CR

'Well, that's true,' said Noel. 'You are very fond of Agatha Christie.'

He and Sylvie had gathered a couple of days later in Caitlin's flat, and Sylvie dutifully recounted her visit to Mary. 'That was it,' she said. 'When I asked her about his diabetes she just changed the subject—the woman was close to tears. I don't think she knows anything—but she knows there's something not right about the story. Maybe she suspects he was killed, and she can't face it.'

'Do you think that's why she wanted a quick cremation?' asked Caitlin.

Sylvie looked at Caitlin. 'That would make sense—if she suspected anything there would have to be an autopsy, and she'd want to avoid that. It would mean the whole story of Pomfrey being in a gay sauna would come out, and she would hate that.'

'Or she suspects who did it and she's covering up for them?' said Noel, thinking aloud.

'OK,' said Caitlin, who was enjoying the exercise more than she suspected she should. She took out a big piece of butcher's paper and a couple of felt pens: 'Let's plot what we have.'

'Rahid,' said Noel firmly, 'is definitely hiding something.'

Caitlin drew a set of squares on the paper, names down the side, Means/Motive/Opportunity headings across the top.

'Means?' asked Sylvie sceptically.

'The insulin,' said Caitlin. She looked at Noel. 'The vial your friend found was empty, right? It would have had enough to kill someone if it were injected into them.'

'But,' said Sylvie, 'how do you inject someone without their consent?'

'It's possible.' Noel shuddered, imagining the scene. 'If Pomfrey—if he were already naked, lying down and someone crept into the cubicle—if they knew what they were doing it would be over before he realised.'

'Right,' said Caitlin, 'so anyone who was in the sauna that night could have done it. But motives?'

'Why Rahid?' asked Sylvie, 'why would he want to kill Pomfrey?'

'He hated him,' said Caitlin reluctantly. 'He thought Pomfrey had blocked his career.'

'What about the sauna owner, Joe?' asked Caitlin. 'He could do it easily—but what motive would he have?'

'I don't know,' said Noel. 'But I think he's hiding something. Maybe he and Rahid were in it together?'

Caitlin wrote both names on the paper, which was spread across her dining table, one corner slightly moist from a drop of olive oil. 'Alejandro?' she asked.

'No,' said Sylvie. 'He only came to the house after the body was brought back.'

'I'm not sure,' said Noel. 'Winston said Alejandro might have been at the sauna earlier that evening. And certifying the death would be a perfect way of covering it up, if he was the killer.'

'Motive?' asked Caitlin, her pen hovering over the paper. 'I know things between him and Pomfrey were tense. But surely that's not enough?'

'Put him down,' said Sylvie. 'There might be something we don't know—he's very jumpy whenever Pomfrey's death is mentioned.'

'So when the body was found,' said Caitlin, thinking aloud, 'the manager—Joe—called Spencer. But why?'

'I imagine he knew he was organising the Conference with Pomfrey,' said Sylvie. 'But if he only came to the sauna after the body was found—'

'We don't know that,' said Noel. 'Maybe he'd been there earlier—like Alejandro. Shouldn't we try to find out?'

Sylvie agreed. 'I think Spencer might have been hiding something from Pomfrey, something to do with Trust finances. I think I need another talk with Elvira.'

'I could ask Winston,' said Noel. 'Maybe he can remember seeing him there.'

'Winston is also a suspect,' said Caitlin. 'Yes I know,' she continued, before Noel could object. 'He's been giving you information all along. But maybe that's a double bluff, maybe he did it and he needs to show off how clever he was.'

'But he wouldn't have known Pomfrey,' said Noel. 'What possible motive—?' He stopped, suddenly remembering Winston talking about going with older men for money. 'No, I'm sure it's not him.'

'It's absurd,' said Sylvie. 'Maybe it's like *Murder on the Orient Express* and they all did it.'

'Or none of them,' said Caitlin. 'It could be someone we don't know about. This isn't a closed room in a snowbound house where we know everyone who could have had access to Pomfrey that night.' She looked at Noel. 'Can we trust you to question Winston about who else might have been there without letting him know he might be a suspect?'

Noel nodded. They stared at the paper, the five names neatly written with ticks and question marks for motive and opportunity. Only Rahid seemed to meet all three criteria, but as Sylvie had pointed out he was the one who had first suggested murder.

'Next steps?' asked Caitlin, her pen hovering. 'I guess we should try to find out who was in the sauna the night Pomfrey died—Noel, that's your job. If either Alejandro or Spencer were definitely there we can add them as real suspects. Maybe I could find out more about Alejandro's disagreement with Pomfrey.'

Sylvie sighed. 'I guess,' she said, 'I'll try to find out why Spencer was called in that night. And whether he had any connection with the sauna.'

'And the sauna owner, Joe,' said Noel. 'How do we tackle him?'

Sylvie thought. Presumably it was Joe who had called Spencer to the sauna after finding the body, which made sense if he knew who Pomfrey was. But if he did, was that in itself a clue? Was there perhaps some connection between Joe and Pomfrey that needed to be hidden—and if so, how would they discover it?

'Caitlin,' she said, 'you need to talk to Rahid. I know he's a suspect—but he's also the most likely to know what Joe was up to.'

Caitlin nodded. Just as Noel was convinced that Winston was innocent, she felt the same about Rahid. Enthusiastically she added another column: she would tackle Rahid and then Alejandro; Sylvie would investigate Spencer and whether he had any motive to want Pomfrey out of the way; Noel would follow up with Winston. Tentatively she put a question mark beside Joe, confident that Rahid would give her a lead.

There seemed little more to be said, and after an awkward half hour over wine and cheese they parted, each of them hovering between excitement and apprehension. Sylvie was still sceptical, though certain there was more to Pomfrey's death than they knew; Noel was determined both to find out what happened and to prove that Winston was not involved; Caitlin was enjoying her deepening friendship with Sylvie and unravelling what had happened.

21

Rahid battled through the narrow entry to the Opera House, wondering what he was doing surrounded by people for whom he basically felt contempt. As usual the audience was overwhelmingly white, very different to the world in which he had grown up. But once inside the magic of *Lammermoor* took over, and, predictably, the famous sextet brought tears, which he sniffled away, embarrassed that Caitlin might notice. They made their way slowly down the stairs from the upper balcony, sparring good-naturedly over whether it was possible to see Lucia as anything other than a stereotypical female victim.

A few streets away they found a small café with two very cramped seats at the back. A surly waitress took their order, ignoring Rahid and only looking at Caitlin. Rahid was used to such snubs and usually laughed them off, but they hurt nonetheless.

'What the fuck are we doing here?' he mused, still smarting from the waitress. 'An Asian gay and an ace feminist watching yet another hetero romantic fantasy.'

'Maybe,' said Caitlin, 'but it's hardly realistic. Isn't *bel canto* opera camp by definition?'

'At least it's not as bad as ballet. All those determinedly heterosexual couplings dancing on pointed toes to the music of Tchaikovsky, who was clearly queer.'

'The only time I went to the ballet,' said Caitlin, 'I kept waiting for them to sing. It felt oddly incomplete.'

'But ballet is all about respectable perving: we get to see beautiful bodies contorting in skin-tight clothes and pretend it's high art. Half the audience only come to check out the codpieces.'

'Or get off on the girls' legs,' said Cailin scornfully. 'But ballet—classical ballet—is ridiculous and cruel. It destroys young girls' bodies and leaves them crippled before they reach thirty.'

A different waiter returned and placed both orders in front of Caitlin. Looking at him Rahid took his plate of pasta and moved it closer, knocking a fork to the ground. 'I need another fork, mate,' he said, looking directly at the waiter. The waiter turned and hurried off.

'Rahid,' said Caitlin, 'what you said at dinner—do you really think Pomfrey was murdered?'

'Yes,' said Rahid, 'masked men broke into the sauna and stabbed him three times … seriously Caitlin, I don't know. Men do have sudden heart attacks you know.'

Caitlin looked at him. 'You know there was an empty insulin bottle in his room,' she said. 'And it turns out Pomfrey was not diabetic. Someone could have walked in and injected him. That could be fatal.'

Rahid scowled, annoyed that Winston had not taken his advice to say nothing about finding the bottle. 'Look,' he said, 'it's a pretty far-fetched conjecture. Can't you just let it go?'

'We know you and Joe were in the sauna that night—oh, and Winston too, he found the body. Or says he did. Do you know whether Alejandro or Spencer were there?'

Rahid swirled the dregs of his coffee and said nothing. Caitlin persisted. 'You realise,' she said, 'you could be a suspect. Don't you want to help us clear this up?'

Rahid looked at her, and she saw he was scared. 'Leave it,' he said. 'You might get into trouble.' He stood up, wanting to leave. 'But yes,' he said, 'Alejandro was there that evening. Not sure about Spencer—I've seen him there in the past. He seemed to have a key to get in through the back entrance, don't know why.'

Caitlin scrambled to get her things together.

'Walk you to the tube,' said Rahid. 'And no more murder talk, right?'

They walked through the crowded streets to Tottenham Court, rode together in silence down the long escalators pointing them towards Ealing and Ruslip, pushing their way through evening revellers to get on the Central line. He left her to change lines at Oxford Circus with a quick kiss, and she mulled over the conversation, convinced he was hiding something. Rahid had suddenly remembered something, and he was not at all sure what it might reveal.

○◦

That weekend the tennis club was hosting its biannual Mix-n-Smash Social Sunday, and Caitlin decided to roster herself on a game with Alejandro. She arrived early and looked for Matthew, the tennis coach and general organiser. He was sitting on the porch, drinking a large smoothie and frowning over several large pieces of paper as he tried to match up players. The rules of the social event required a rotation of mixed doubles, with no prizes and an early supper to follow. Because normal competitions were suspended for the day it was hoped that members would feel less compulsion to win, but the very absence of formal competition seemed to make several even more determined. 'That one,' he said, pointing at a name, 'he's so set on winning he can literally push his partner off the court going for the ball.' He looked curiously at Caitlin. 'But if you want me to match you up with Professor Herrera, no problem. Just watch out, he can lose his cool pretty easily.'

Caitlin decided that if they won their first round she might have the chance to question Alejandro in the break. They were lucky in the draw, coming up against a particularly ill-matched couple who bickered over every dropped shot, and won easily.

Walking off the court Caitlin took a deep breath. 'Alejandro,' she said, 'are you sure Pomfrey died from a heart attack?'

He stopped and glared at her. 'What is this?' he asked. 'Are you questioning my medical expertise?'

'Of course not.' Caitlin floundered, not sure what she could say. 'But we know he didn't die at home—and perhaps, if something happened at the sauna—'

'The sauna? I know the one you mean and I believe Pomfrey might have been there before he died. But that means nothing.'

'And you—were you there?'

'I have been there to supervise a behavioural research project. Not as often as Pomfrey I believe.'

'But that evening—?'

'Certainly not.' They were standing together at the edge of one of the courts and Alejandro became aware that several of the players were looking at them. 'That's all I have to say on the matter,' he said. 'I resent whatever implications you're making. If you want to ask questions maybe you should ask whether Pomfrey was involved in drug trafficking at that place.'

He turned and stalked up the stairs to the clubhouse. Caitlin waited, wondering what to make of that last comment. She already knew that Alejandro had sparred with Pomfrey, but it seemed there was more than disagreement over the vaccine trials involved. Rahid had been certain Alejandro had been in the sauna that evening; if he was right she could now list Alejandro under all three columns: means, motive, opportunity. As a doctor it would have been comparatively easy for him to get hold of insulin, and to inject Pomfrey. She decided to call Sylvie that evening and fill her in. 'See what you can find out from Spencer,' she said. 'And why he was the person called in when the body was discovered.'

22

Sylvie was seated at her desk, poring over the apparently endless paper trail left behind by the Conference, when Elvia arrived, gave her a half smile and went into Spencer's office.

Spencer greeted her effusively, pointing to the black armchair, then seated himself strategically behind his desk, his computer open and facing her as if to signal he had nothing to hide.

'As you can see,' he said, using the sort of confidential tones with which a doctor might impart a disturbing diagnosis, 'there were some large transfers of money that are not always straight forward. The Conference, of course, meant we were handling large sums. But here'—he highlighted one line—'there seems to be an agreement with a particular organisation that perhaps was a little outside our remit.'

'Mary's charity?'

'I am investigating,' said Spencer. 'If there's anything irregular I shall find it and close it off.' He cleared his throat. 'The investment accounts are more complex. Pomfrey might have made some choices that were, shall we say, unwise. But I'm looking into them.'

Elvira nodded. 'I would appreciate being kept informed,' she said. 'I go back to Oslo soon. And I need to discuss this with my fellow trustees.'

'Of course.' Spencer's tone grew yet more ingratiating. 'I

wonder,' he said, 'whether you have considered that you might be the appropriate person to replace Pomfrey.'

Elvira said nothing but gave him a slight smile. She stood up. 'I hope,' she said, making for the door, 'you will have more details of these investments before I have to return to Norway?'

As soon as she'd left, Sylvie went into Spencer's office carrying a set of papers that needed his attention. Oddly, winding up the Conference seemed to involve more work than the preparation: the stream of invoices, reports, acquittals, certifications of attendance seemed endless.

'Yes,' said Spencer, 'lots for us to tidy up. Pomfrey was more of a big picture man, not always on top of all the details.'

Sylvie looked at him. 'Spencer,' she asked, 'why were you called into the sauna the night he died? Did Joe know something?'

'Know something? He knew us both through the Conference—Spartacus was a sponsor. And he understood the need for discretion.'

'And he knew how to find you? Don't you live on the other side of town?'

'I was free—quick drive, that time of night.' He was becoming impatient. 'What is this interrogation about, Sylvie?'

She took a deep breath, unsure how much to say.

'It's possible,' she said slowly, 'that Pomfrey's death was less straightforward than we thought.'

'Nonsense,' said Spencer confidently. 'Heart attack. Not really surprising given where he was. I don't want to pass judgment but if he hadn't been engaging in—not that I know, of course—but what was he doing there late at night? We couldn't let the press get hold of that, it would have destroyed Mary. Maybe moving the body was skirting the law, but I'm sure you can see it was for the best.'

'I've been wondering,' said Sylvie, 'how did the sauna owner know Pomfrey? He must have recognised him to call you in.'

'The research project: both he and Alejandro would have met Joe—' He lowered his voice. 'Confidentially, Pomfrey might have had more to do with the sauna than we know. And not just as a client, if that's the right word for what he was doing there.' He paused. 'I'm not sure where you are going with this, Sylvie. I assure you that if there is anything improper I shall ferret it out. I owe that to the Trust.' He stood up. 'But now I have other things to deal with, as I'm sure you do.'

CB

As soon as Sylvie had left Spencer rang Joe, careful that his office door was shut.

'I'm not happy,' he said abruptly, 'there are too many people asking questions about Pomfrey's death.' He counted them off: Elvira, Sylvie, even Alejandro.

'The one I'm worried about,' replied Joe, 'is that young bloke, Noel. Can't see where he fits in.'

'I don't know him. You don't suppose ...' Spencer thought for a moment. 'Could he be a private dick someone has hired?'

'Pretty clumsy one if he is. But he does need to be dealt with.'

Joe thought for a moment. 'Leave it with me.'

CB

Improper. Sylvie thought about that word as she worked her way through voluminous correspondence about unpaid extras on hotel bills and cabs. She had a vague memory of something Pomfrey had said one evening, as they were leaving the office, something about improper—no illicit—dealings at Spartacus? They had been working through the proofs of the Conference program, with its elaborate acknowledgments of sponsors and partners, and she had asked him about Spartacus, a business name she didn't recognise. He grimaced and made an off-hand comment that she wished now she could remember. But at the time it had seemed unimportant, Spartacus was just one of a number of small businesses that had been cajoled into lending support to the Conference.

CB

Breaking the connection with Mary's organisation, thought Spencer, would require some finesse. What he did not know, or had perhaps forgotten, was that Elvira knew Mary and was likely to ask her directly about any connection she might have had with the Trust.

As soon as she'd left the office Elvira called Mary and invited her to lunch the following day. She had planned to visit St Martins in the Fields to book for a choral concert and suggested a small restaurant nearby, close to Charing Cross station.

Elvira was already seated and sipping a glass of wine when Mary arrived, flustered and looking slightly unkempt. They air-kissed and spent some time deciding what to eat, settling for salads. Mary took a couple of tentative bites at a bread roll, kneading it into a crumpled mess.

'I know your organisation has been advocating abstinence in Africa,' said Elvira quietly. 'Are you sure this is the most effective message?'

'Absolutely,' said Mary. 'If we can stop promiscuity we can stop the spread of HIV.'

'That wasn't Pomfrey's view?'

'We disagreed.' Mary clasped at the remnants of her roll. 'Yes, we argued about that.'

'So Pomfrey wasn't helping to fund your work—through the Trust?'

'Of course not. He was furious when he discovered that Spencer—' She stopped, aware she had said too much. 'That is, Spencer understands how important *God Loves Us All* can be in the fight against HIV.' She leant over her uneaten salad. 'Confidentially,' she said, 'he would like me to replace Pomfrey as chair of the Trust.'

Elvira nodded, wondering whom else Spencer might have approached. 'Please try to eat, my dear,' she said gently, 'it's important you keep your strength up.'

Mary, she thought, would be totally inappropriate as chair, but no need to tell her that now.

'Mary,' she asked, 'you wrote to Pomfrey as Righteous, didn't you?'

'I tried to talk to him about stopping homosexuals and how their promiscuity was spreading the virus. He got so angry with me that it was pointless.' She sighed. 'But he guessed the messages came from me. He told me that if I didn't stop this nonsense he would leave me.'

'But you didn't stop?'

Mary twirled a piece of arugula onto her fork and let it hang mid-air. 'Elvira,' she asked, 'did Pomfrey ever talk to you about being involved in an affair?'

'No,' said Elvira firmly, 'and I don't think—'

'I have to tell someone.' Mary's voice trembled. 'There was a young man—I'm sure of it. I know it's crazy, but I keep thinking of them together and I hate him.'

'Because he's a man? Would you feel differently were it a woman?'

Mary sighed, on the verge of tears. 'Yes,' she said quietly. 'But that's wrong of me isn't it?'

'Why do you feel so threatened by homosexuals Mary?'

'I think I always feared that Pomfrey—that he would find satisfaction that I couldn't give him. I suppose I always knew there was that side of him, but he held it in. Till recently.' She rubbed her eyes, 'If he left me—the shame of it—I would have felt my life was a failure.'

'You loved him?'

'Yes,' whispered Mary. 'That's what made it all so hard.'

23

Noel had decided not to ask Winston if he could stay with him, but Maurice at *The Brigadoon* was effusive in his welcome. 'Down here again to see the boy?' he asked, almost rubbing his hands together in celebration. 'We'll have to buy you a season ticket.'

He led Noel up the stairs to a room at the back of the house. 'Smaller than last time, I fear,' he said. 'We have a lovely Scottish lad in the room you stayed in last time. But do feel free to bring your friend back if you wish.' He threw open the small window, which looked out onto a narrow lane filled with rubbish bins. 'No sea view,' he said. 'But the only noise is on garbage nights.'

Noel nodded, then decided to go in search of Winston. They had a vague plan to meet in a small pub near the beachfront where Joe had found a job for Winston. The pub was a ramshackle three-storey umber brick building overlooking the less fashionable side of the promenade, and Noel found him behind the main bar, polishing glasses. Apart from two solitary men, crouched over beer glasses, the pub was empty, with a slightly desolate air of stale beer and sweat. Winston dropped his polishing rag and lent over the counter to give Noel a kiss.

'Mate,' he said, 'you got here.'

'Staying overnight. When do you get off?'

'I can take a break now. But then working this evening—could go late.' Winston wiped down his hands and came out from behind the counter. 'Let's grab a quick coffee now before the boss comes back.'

They walked to a small building at the end of the road, an old working-class café which was grumbling into gentility with an Italian coffee machine and a couple of vegetarian options chalked on the board above the bar.

'Winston,' said Noel, 'I need you to think back to the night Pomfrey died. Can you remember who you saw in the sauna that night?'

Winston grinned. 'You know,' he said, 'when you work there you don't really notice the punters. 'Cept the occasional really hot one—don't remember anyone like that though. Joe's been at me as well, wanting to know anything I might remember.' He paused, thinking. 'It was leather night ... usually the guys would wear leather vests or jockstraps—I remember there was one who seemed in full leather gear, which was odd, it would be really hot and sticky.'

'You knew Alejandro, the doctor who worked with Pomfrey— they were running the survey together? Do you think he was there?'

'No idea. You think he had something to do with the death?'

'Perhaps. You don't know how long Pomfrey was at Spartacus before you discovered the body?'

'Nah.' Winston looked hard at Noel. 'You think someone did him in, don't you?'

Noel sighed. 'Yes. But it's not like an Agatha Christie mystery, with all the suspects conveniently marooned on a desert island or cut off by a huge storm. Sounds like anyone could have got at him that night, maybe someone we haven't even thought of.'

Winston reached over and held Noel's hands. 'He meant a lot to you, didn't he, the old bloke?'

Noel nodded. 'Yes,' he said. 'He was the most important person in my life.' He paused. 'Somehow I don't think I realised that till he died.'

Winston winked at him and stood up. 'Got to get back, matey,' he said. 'The pub.'

'See you later?'

'Not sure if I'm free. Maybe we should cool it a bit, yeah?'

Noel returned to *The Brigadoon* feeling rejected and alone. Maurice greeted him and immediately invited him to a run through of the play, which was taking longer to produce than he had anticipated. 'People often forget Miss Prism,' he said. 'But she is absolutely vital to the story. Her handbag is really the lynchpin to the whole denouement.'

The theatre group had gathered in a small hall a mile or so along the promenade towards Rottingdean, in what seemed a largely neglected addition to the local church. They arrived just as the rest of the cast were settling into their roles: two younger women, friends of the director, would play Gwendolen and Cecily, while the director would stand in for the two manservants. Noel was struck by the difference between the two women, one of whom was a willowy blonde, with a sullen look, the other much darker, with a rounded figure and a permanent nervous smile. He was introduced to several middle-aged men who would portray John, Algernon and the Canon, all of whom looked interchangeable.

'And our star,' gushed Maurice. 'Roger—otherwise known as Lady Bracknell.'

Roger was a thin man with both receding hair and chin, but he had a deep baritone voice and once in character he became the autocratic Lady Bracknell. As he grew more indignant towards Maurice—Miss Prism—he seemed to grow in stature, and to dominate the reading. Maurice, whose attempt at a feminine voice only produced unnecessary sibilants, was literally trembling with excitement over the final exposition. 'The *Brighton* line,' he expostulated, breaking into giggles, which reappeared as he enthusiastically embraced the actor playing Canon Chasuble.

'Good,' said the director, as Jack, the younger and broader of the men, read the final line. 'Now can we assume you will all know your lines and we can dispense with reading next time?'

The cast dispersed, except for the man who had played Algernon who walked back with Maurice and Noel. Their companion offered to take Noel to a small party in nearby Hove—'just a few friends, very intimate if you know what I mean'—but Noel knew exactly what he meant and declined. Back at *The Brigadoon* he had a quick glass of wine with Maurice and retreated to bed.

ଓ

The next morning Noel got up early and returned to London. He was standing on the platform at Euston, waiting to change to the Northern line, when he felt a hard push from behind, and slipped in the direction of the tracks, falling against a woman who was clutching several shopping bags. Shocked he pulled himself up and looked around, but the train was just pulling in and there were too many people to see anyone who might have shoved him. Shaking, he climbed on board and as soon as he arrived home he rang Sylvie.

'It's got to be intentional,' he said. 'This doesn't happen twice without it meaning something.'

'And you're sure you were pushed? You didn't slip?'

'No,' said Noel. 'I was standing still. How could I have slipped?'

'But who ...?' Sylvie thought. 'You saw Winston yesterday. Do you think he would have reported back to Joe?'

'I trust Winston,' said Noel sadly. 'Even if he doesn't want a relationship—he's a good man.'

'Maybe you need to report it,' said Sylvie. 'If you've been attacked twice—'

'You don't believe me?'

'I do,' said Sylvie, hiding her concern. 'It just seems so unlikely. Two attacks in the middle of London. I really think you need to talk to Winston.'

He spent much of the day at home, drinking pots of tea and trying to concentrate on a book. After several false starts he rang Winston. He felt awkward broaching the possibility, but Winston was appropriately shocked and sympathetic. 'But,' he said, 'it can't have been Joe, he's here in Brighton—I saw him this morning, about the time you were pushed. That's why I couldn't see you last night sweetie, Joe was in town and wanted to meet. He couldn't decide whether to tell me to avoid you or to find out more about you. How would you feel about that?'

I could like that, thought Noel. But he was too cautious to say so. 'Will you be in London next weekend?' he asked tentatively, 'we could meet at my local …' What he didn't tell Winston is that after the attack he now felt panic if he left his house, and avoided taking the tube where possible.

CB

Joe drove back to London, having told Winston that he needed to convince Noel that Pomfrey's death was a straightforward heart attack, and there was no point in continuing to ask questions. Winston had not told him about finding the insulin bottle, and just said that Noel was grieving and trying to understand what his lover was doing in the sauna that night. Joe, who had a strong suspicion that Pomfrey was there as much to confront him about drugs as he was to have casual sex, decided that encouraging Winston to keep seeing Noel might distract him from asking further questions.

The sauna was quiet that evening, and Joe invited Rahid to join him for a coffee in the small bar area next to reception. A chubby man, his towel slipping down to reveal folds of fat, was the only other person in the lounge, and Joe grumbled at the decline of patronage since the Conference. 'We need more gatherings like that,' he said, 'thousands of blokes away from home and wanting to relax.'

'And lots of them from countries where anything like this would be forbidden.' Rahid looked at Joe, wondering why he had been summonsed. 'Are you still nervous that people are asking about Prof. Lister's death?'

'We can't afford the press getting hold of it—asking questions about the sauna.' Joe shuddered, imagining the headlines. 'It would keep too many punters away.' He was very aware that any press interest might uncover the ways in which drugs were being sold and lead to police inquiries.

'Prof. Lister had been here a couple of times,' said Joe, 'looking around. Then he asked for me—I wasn't around at the time. But, yeah, it made me nervous.'

'What do you think really happened that night?' asked Rahid tentatively.

Joe shrugged. 'Mate,' he said, 'who knows? Maybe his heart just gave out, maybe someone helped it happen. Guess there were a few people who weren't too upset to see the end of him.'

Rahid nodded. Pomfrey's death had helped both him and Alejandro, as well as taking the heat off Joe. He couldn't see an immediate motive for Spencer, but the fact he had colluded in removing the body made him a possible suspect, especially as he seemed to have easy access to the sauna. And Joe, he realised, would have been perfectly placed to attack Pomfrey, as, indeed, had he.

'You saw him that evening, didn't you?' asked Joe. 'Maybe you talked to him?'

Rahid sighed: he was tempted to lie, but he suspected Joe already knew. 'Yes,' he said 'I did talk—well, I yelled at him. He was already undressed, and he walked past the massage room. But a client showed up before he could say anything back. That was my last massage for the evening; I got dressed, had a quick soda and left. I didn't see him again.'

The two men looked at each other, wondering what each might be holding back.

24

'OK,' said Caitlin. 'What have we got?'

She and Sylvie were seated around her dining table, the big piece of butcher's paper in front of them. Caitlin looked at the names and frowned.

'Are you sure,' she said tentatively, 'we shouldn't add Noel? He could easily have followed Pomfrey to the sauna out of jealousy.'

'That's ridiculous!' said Sylvie. 'Why would he have suggested looking into it if he were the murderer?'

'I guess.' Caitlin looked unconvinced. 'It's just such an obvious motive. And it's hard to find anything that strong for the others.'

'Not sure,' said Sylvie. 'I think Alejandro might well have had good reason to hate Pomfrey.'

'They had clashed over the vaccine trials ...'

'I think it's more personal. Alejandro seemed to think Pomfrey was involved in selling drugs—that's ridiculous, I know. But what if he thought he had proof? And there was that odd comment from Spencer. He seemed to imply that Pomfrey was more connected with the sauna than we knew.'

'Do you believe him?'

'I'd be less inclined to trust him than Pomfrey. He's good at hiding stuff, especially financial stuff. But if there was something illegal going on at the sauna, that puts Joe back in the picture. And Rahid.'

Caitlin frowned. 'Rahid knows something,' she said. 'But I'm sure he's not a killer. And he is certain he saw Alejandro in the sauna that evening.'

'Which Alejandro denies,' Sylvie thought. 'We need to confront him head on. But I already tried that at tennis, and it didn't work. What we need is a trap.'

'What if we went to him,' said Caitlin, thinking aloud, 'and said we knew Pomfrey was killed, and we had proof. Then watched his reaction?'

'Or get all of them in a room together and denounce someone. That's what Poirot would do.'

'There is the memorial service later this week,' Caitlin said, 'you're helping arrange that, right?'

'With Mary and Spencer.' Sylvie grimaced. 'Spencer of course thinks big. He wanted to get Elton John to sing.' She stood up, stretched. 'It all revolves around the Spartacus Sauna. I think we need to find out more about that place and what Pomfrey knew about it. And Elvira is the person who can help us. I'll arrange for us to all get together.'

'With Noel?'

Sylvie looked at her. 'So you're ready to cross him off the list of suspects?'

Caitlin nodded. 'You should all come here for supper later this week,' she said, already planning the menu.

◌৪

When Rahid got home from an early night at the sauna he found Justin in the kitchen, heating up left over stroganoff. They kissed, briefly, and Rahid grabbed a beer, stretching out on one of the hard wooden chairs next to their kitchen table.

'Hot men at the sauna tonight?' asked Justin, who enjoyed teasing Rahid about his job.

Rahid grunted. 'Only one client,' he said. 'Joe is clearly worried that business is dropping off.'

'Maybe you need to tell people about the geezer who died there. Nothing like a hint of scandal to get people's attention.' Justin looked at him, mashing the left-over potatoes. 'That day after your Prof. died,' he said, 'you were really upset when you heard. Didn't really make sense to me, you hated the guy.'

'I didn't tell you?—guess I was too scared. I thought I might have killed him.'

Justin looked sceptical. 'You? What, with a knife?'

'I saw him in the sauna that night. I was shocked—I'd never suspected he was into men. I didn't recognise him at first, only wearing a towel, so I followed him to make sure. He didn't seem that interested in what was going on, he just went into an empty cubicle, so I decided to confront him. He was sitting up, seemed half-asleep, and I walked in on him. I said he'd cheated me out of my doctorate, and I would reveal him as a closet case—I lost it, I started yelling—then I realised there were people in the corridor, and I just hissed at him to be careful and left. When I heard he'd died of a heart attack I thought maybe I'd brought it on—and I was afraid someone might have heard us.'

Justin leant over and took his hand. 'He didn't die because of you.'

'I know that now. At least, if Caitlin is right, and he was killed with an injection of insulin, it had nothing to do with me. But if it comes out that we had an argument that evening won't I be the logical suspect?'

'Maybe you should tell the others about your argument with him. If it helps find who really killed Prof. you have nothing to worry about.'

'I think Alejandro is hiding something,' said Rahid thoughtfully. 'Not sure how I can use that, though. But I'd love to see that pompous prig squirm a little.'

Joe spooned leftover potatoes and gravy onto their plates.

'Perhaps it was someone you haven't thought of—someone the Prof. had sex with?' he said.

'I've thought about that. But if it were murder, it was carefully planned. Doesn't that make it more likely to be someone he already knew?'

'I'll ask around,' said Justin. 'See if anyone has heard of the Prof. having secret liaisons with leather men who kill their partners.'

He grinned at Rahid, who seemed unsure whether to take him seriously. Rahid stood up, moved over to Justin and nuzzled his face against the nape of his neck, still fresh from a recent haircut. 'Love you,' he said, but he felt Justin tense, and he quickly withdrew. Later, looking back on that day, he knew that was the moment Justin had decided to leave him.

∞

Winston showed up on time, wearing ripped jeans and a denim jacket with pink epaulettes. Noel had decided to avoid the *Black Cap*, which was likely to be crowded in anticipation of the evening's drag show, and they were sitting in a small pub off Upper Street, a russet-brown brick building topped with a row of small attic windows, which Noel liked for its counter meals. Winston gave him a big smooch and Noel leapt back, unsure how to interpret it.

'Are you here because Joe told you to be?' he asked. 'Or did you really want to see me?'

Winston poked his tongue at Noel, throwing himself onto a bench. 'Could be both matey,' he said. 'Nah, it's good to see you.'

They chatted for a few minutes, choosing food and drink, discussing the trains from Brighton and the ease of using the new Oyster card on the tube. Winston was planning to take his mother to her doctor on Monday, and he grumbled about a sister who lived a few streets away but was always too busy to help.

The food arrived—two plates of fish, chips and mashed peas, and Noel decided he needed to ask: 'Have you remembered anything more from that night?'

Winston frowned. 'You know,' he said carefully, 'I think there was one thing. Remember I told you about the geezer in full leather?—jacket, cap, the whole outfit, and how that looked odd? He seemed to be avoiding people, but I think I saw him go upstairs to the cubicles when I was cleaning the corridors.'

'So he could have gone into the cubicle where Pomfrey was?'

'Easily. But so could anyone else who was around that evening.'

'This guy: did you recognise him?'

'That's it,' said Winston, frowning, 'I only saw him from behind, for a moment like. I noticed him because of the leather gear, but there was something that felt wrong. He didn't look as if he was used to being in a sauna, seemed as if he was avoiding looking at people as he passed them. Pretty sure whoever it was felt pretty uncomfortable being there.'

'Maybe,' said Noel, 'that was the person who killed Pomfrey, and the leather was to hide his identity. Maybe—'

'Matey,' said Winston, 'let it go. Even if your man was there that night it doesn't mean he loved you any less.'

'And if someone killed him? Don't you think I have a right to know who? And why?'

'In our world,' said Winston carefully, 'sometimes it's better not to know too much. It can only get you into trouble.' He licked the last crumbs from his fork. 'So, want to come with me to a rave? There's a small one happening down past Waterloo.'

Noel flinched. 'Not really my scene,' he said, conscious of the gap between them. 'I'm tired,' he said, meaning he wasn't prepared to cross the city and stay up all night for the uncertain pleasure of Winston's company at the end. He would go home alone and find comfort in a book, missing the certainty he'd felt with Pomfrey that now seemed to have been a romantic illusion.

ଔ

'That doesn't help much,' said Sylvie, after Noel recounted his conversation with Winston. 'Though it does rather point to Alejandro or Spencer.'

They were seated again around the table: Sylvie, Caitlin, Noel and Elvira.

Caitlin had settled on a different pasta dish, this time, linguini with clams in a vague nod to Elvira's presumed Norwegian taste for seafood. The others had brought wine and desserts and, given the reason for the dinner, they were remarkably lightheaded.

Elvira regaled them with stories of working in a number of developing countries, and her encounter with a former Queen of Sikkim. At one point she mentioned her last meeting with Pomfrey in Oslo, and Caitlin quickly filled her in on their suspicions so far.

Elvira nodded. 'Yes,' she said, 'I had the feeling after talking to Mary that there was more to Pomfrey's death than she was saying. And you are sure he was killed in the sauna?'

'We can't be sure,' said Noel. 'But there is the empty insulin bottle. And Winston swears his glasses weren't there, which means someone was in the cubicle and took them before his body was discovered.'

'The problem is there were lots of people around—and no-one seems to have seen anything.' Sylvie sighed. 'Joe, Rahid—the resident masseur—and we think Alejandro was there, though he denies it.'

'And Spencer,' added Caitlin. 'We know he turned up to help move the body—but he could easily have been there earlier. Seems he knew his way around the sauna.'

Elvira looked at her. 'Now why does that not surprise me?' she said ironically. 'Do you know the meaning of a special purpose vehicle?'

All three shook their heads. 'It seems,' said Elvira, 'that Spencer had established such a vehicle to invest some of the Trust's money. And that some of that money had been invested in the Spartacus Sauna. He suggested it was Pomfrey's doing, but I think it was Spencer who handled investments for the Trust.'

'Pomfrey was very vague about money,' said Noel eagerly. 'He said he'd grown up knowing he had enough, and he left others to worry about managing it.'

'I still think Alejandro is the most likely suspect,' said Sylvie. 'He hated Pomfrey. And we know he can be volatile, Caitlin and I have seen him at tennis.'

Elvira looked sceptical. 'I know he disliked Pomfrey,' she said carefully. 'But would that be sufficient reason?'

'It would be if he thought Pomfrey was involved in pushing drugs,' said Sylvie. 'Though frankly I think it's more likely he was tracking down whoever was responsible.'

'Don't forget Joe,' said Noel, remembering the attacks on him. 'If anyone was involved selling drugs at the sauna it had to be him. I know Winston said he couldn't have been at the tube station when I was attacked, but he could have had someone follow me.'

Elvira had not heard about the two possible attacks on Noel, and he filled her in. She nodded, unsure how that fitted any of their suspects.

'We know Joe didn't want me asking questions,' said Noel. 'Maybe he was using the sauna to push drugs, and Pomfrey had discovered it? It would be pretty easy for him to move around the sauna and not be noticed.'

'Or Rahid?' Sylvie said, looking apologetically at Caitlin. Caitlin shook her head slowly but said nothing.

'Have you shared your suspicions with Mary?' asked Elvira gently.

'I tried.' Sylvie remembered her last visit to Mary, and how upset she seemed. 'But she refused to talk about it.'

'Mary has invited me to tea before I go home,' said Elvira. 'Maybe I can ask her.'

⋈

'I've made scones.'

Elvira had arrived at the house in Highgate on a hot afternoon and felt uncomfortable after a brisk walk from the tube. Mary, she noticed, was wearing a multicoloured caftan, which seemed oddly inappropriate for the weather.

'Do take a couple,' said Mary, producing a tray of scones which seemed to be both over- and under-cooked, along with two pots of jam and a saucer of cream. Mary poured out the tea, her hands shaking. 'Now,' she said, 'it's very important that you get the order right: jam first, cream on top.'

Elvira smiled. 'How very British of you,' she said. 'Tea and scones.' She looked hard at Mary, who seemed to have put on weight in the past weeks. Maybe that explained the caftan.

'My dear,' she said, 'is there anything about Pomfrey's death you haven't told me?'

Mary's hand shook, and a gobbet of cream fell onto the carpet.

'People talk,' said Elvira. 'I know he died in a gay sauna.' Mary started to say something, but Elvira continued. 'I promise you it's not going to become public. But some of your friends are wondering whether there may have been—' she hesitated, looking for the right words— 'foul play, I think is the expression.'

Mary seized her cup so hard it threatened to crack. 'Pomfrey died of a heart attack,' she said softly, 'I swear it. Yes, he didn't die at home, and I'm grateful to Spencer for bringing him here, but that was just to avoid the police—and the media—better for everyone if he died at home.'

'Is that why you arranged a rapid cremation?'

Mary's hands were shaking. 'Yes,' she said. 'I was afraid that someone might have seen him at the sauna and would ask questions. He was an important scientist, Elvira. If people found out where he died that's what he'd be remembered for.'

'And your charity work would be affected?'

'There was a lot at stake. Spencer understood that. And the owner—Joe. He could see it as well.'

Of course, thought Elvira, the last thing Joe would have wanted would be a dead body leading to police and press interest in Spartacus.

25

The memorial service took place the following Thursday, in the convention centre which had recently housed the Conference. A motor home exhibition had already moved in, but one large hall was available, an ornate room with gold chandeliers and heavy brocade curtains. Spencer and Sylvie had enlisted several of the younger lab staff to assist in organising the event, and they stood at the entrance registering names as several hundred people showed up. Most of them were work colleagues of Pomfrey's, but his had been a long and distinguished career, and the crowd ranged from several members of Parliament to a group of leather-jacketed ACT UP members. At least one potential Nobel laureate was present— Spencer rushed over to shake her hand as she entered inconspicuously with a small group from the Pasteur Institute— along with several of his Highgate neighbours, more expensively dressed than most.

Mary sat in the front row, dressed in a new grey frock which seemed slightly too tight, surrounded by several heads of universities and teaching hospitals; immediately behind them were Spencer, Alejandro, Elvira and Sylvie. Caitlin and Rahid sat together halfway towards the back; Noel had arrived early, watched as people arrived, then taken a seat at the very back of the room from where he could leave unseen. A small group of singers from the Regents Park Choral Society were grouped in front of a large vase of lilies, ready to open the event with a selection from Handel's *The ways of Zion do mourn*.

Noel looked at the elaborately printed booklet, with the long list of speakers—a leading medico from St Vincent's Hospital in Sydney; someone from the Terrence Higgins Trust; a Deputy Secretary from the Department of Health—and thought how little any of them really knew about Pomfrey. Planning a reconciliation with Alejandro, Spencer had added him to the program, asking him to speak about the search for an HIV vaccine. Noel, however, was no longer in the hall to hear him announce that his lab was about to commence human trials; as the first speaker reached the fourth of what had promised to be his penultimate point he quietly stood up and left. As he walked through the hallways he could hear muttered applause and the first strains of a choral work. He had shut the shop for the afternoon, but he decided to go back and ground himself in sorting out new consignments.

There was something refreshing about coming up from the station at Camden Town and breathing fresh air; it was a humid afternoon, with a faint hint of smog in an otherwise cloudless sky. A few buskers were sitting around the station entrance, and Noel put a coin in one of their caps. He entered the shop from the back and pulled up the shutters, disturbing a sleeping man who had rolled his blankets under the awning; the man slowly gathered his belongings. Almost immediately two young women came into the shop to browse and were soon giggling over a set of old schoolgirl stories, books Mrs Mackie referred to as *jolly hockey sticks*.

The door opened again, and Joe walked in. Noel looked up from behind the counter, startled.

'Don't worry mate,' said Joe, walking towards him. 'Not going to hurt you.' He looked round the shop. 'Nice place you've got here,' he said approvingly. 'Might buy something myself.'

'But that's not why you're here?' Noel came out from behind the counter, suddenly energised. 'What do you want?'

'Look,' said Joe, lowering his voice in case he was overheard, 'I get it that you're upset that your fella died. But he's not the first man to have a heart attack in a sauna. No one benefits if you keep asking questions.'

'And what if he was murdered?'

'Now that's quite an accusation. Can you prove it?'

Noel hesitated, unsure how much Joe knew.

'You see mate,' said Joe, 'that sort of language gets us all into trouble. If you had real proof you'd have taken it to the cops by now.'

He turned and flicked through a stack of books that sat near the counter. 'I'll take this one,' he said, handing a history of the Tudors to Noel. 'Those Henrys,' he said, 'they knew how to manage troublemakers. People always talk about Henry VIII, but it was his dad who set things up for him.'

He reached into his wallet for a ten-pound note. 'Here,' he said, 'keep the change. Ever want to visit Spartacus tell them it's on me.' He winked and walked out.

One of the girls came up to the counter with an early edition of *The Schoolgirls Own Annual* and spent several minutes searching for her credit card.

CB

The memorial service ended with a message from Downing Street, which focused on self-congratulations for Britain's role in creating the Millennium Development Goals, and the chorus came on stage to sing an extract from Elgar's *Nimrod*. A carefully selected group made their way to an adjoining room with a plush deep blue carpet, where refreshments had been laid out and Spencer took the opportunity to corner Elvira.

'Have you finished your inquiries?' he asked, somewhat nervously.

'The Trustees,' she said, 'are meeting by teleconference on Monday. I hope we can resolve matters and I can go home then.'

Spencer gulped. 'But,' he said, 'shouldn't I be part of that conversation. As chief executive, I mean—'

'We didn't feel it necessary,' said Elvira. 'I've asked Sylvie to arrange the meeting.' She turned to greet a former colleague, making clear the conversation was over.

Caitlin came up to Sylvie, who was looking distractedly at the serving tables, wondering whether they had over-catered and what to do with left-over pastries. 'This is our opportunity,' said Caitlin, pointing at Alejandro. 'We could ask him straight out whether he did it.'

She took Sylvie by the arm and moved towards Alejandro. Seeing them he gave a slight bow, then turned away.

'Professor,' said Caitlin determinedly, 'you really didn't like Pomfrey Lister very much, did you?'

Alejandro looked at her, uncertain how to respond. 'No,' he said slowly, 'no, I respected him. But he was a very arrogant man under all that charm.'

'And you disagreed over the research?'

'Pomfrey resented the fact that I had cracked a problem. He wanted to be sure he kept control, even if his assumptions proved unsuccessful.'

'Did you know,' asked Sylvie suddenly, 'That Pomfrey was diabetic?'

'Yes, Mary told me. I didn't know until the night he died. But someone was talking about diabetes recently—maybe Spencer?'

'We believe Pomfrey was murdered,' said Sylvie. 'Someone injected him with a massive dose of insulin and dropped the vial. You were in the sauna that night?'

'I was close, yes. I was visiting my—I had to call in at a centre near Shoreditch.' He frowned. 'Murdered?—no, that's ridiculous. It was his heart.' He glared at them. 'I suggest you drop this absurd line of questioning immediately. It will do neither of you any good.'

Shaken, Alejandro left the hall. Any inquiry about Pomfrey's death would inevitably involve him, possibly bring in the police. He had visions of interrogations; of the shame his wife would feel were he involved in a murder inquiry. His disagreements with Pomfrey were well known, suspicion would inevitably fall on him. He remembered his discussion with Joe, and Joe's hints that he might have been responsible for Pomfrey's death. He realised he should have been much firmer in his rebuttal.

The room was emptying gradually, leaving those with nothing better to do and those who felt obliged to stay. Mary was standing with a small group of friends and neighbours when Spencer came over and took her aside. They sat on a small bench that ran alongside the hall, under low stainless-steel windows that looked out onto the street.

'I've thought about your idea,' said Mary, 'merging my organisation with the Trust. There would need to be no interference in our work, of course.'

'Indeed,' said Spencer. 'Though I think that might be difficult—the Trustees don't seem disposed to agree to expansion at this point.'

'But if I were to replace Pomfrey?'

Spencer coughed, thinking how best to disillusion her. 'Mary,' he said, 'it's not possible. Things have come to light since we spoke that make it important we distance ourselves from Pomfrey's time as chair. He was an inspiration, of course, but he also made some bad judgments, and we need to move on.'

'Bad judgements? But it was you who provided funds for *God Loves Us All*. Pomfrey was furious when he found out.'

'Best not to discuss those,' said Spencer nervously. 'But there were other investments—I'm trying to sort it out.'

Mary stood up, clearly angry. 'Spencer,' she said, 'I thought we were working together. I thought you understood how important my organisation is for defending young women against the epidemic. Are you saying there will be no more funds?'

Spencer nodded. 'I'm sorry,' he said.

Mary turned and walked off, brushing aside several acquaintances eager to share their memories of Pomfrey. She went into the foyer, loud with the business of motor homes, and found a deserted corner, half hidden behind a huge display for caravan parks on the Sussex Downs. She felt as if everything around her was collapsing. For most of her life Mary had been too self-confident to worry, but that confidence was seeping out of her, even as she put on weight while eating less and less. Even routine events, like shopping or taking the tube, raised anxieties she had never experienced.

CB

The next day Alejandro met Spencer in his office. It was a balmy summer morning, with just a hint of a coming storm, and the building was almost deserted, which suited both men. The meeting was Spencer's idea; despite his vague dislike for Alejandro, whom he thought of as pompous and prone to outbursts of temper, he now seemed a safer choice to succeed Pomfrey than either Mary or Elvira. Elvira's mention of a Trustees meeting from which he was excluded was troubling. He needed to move fast and spend the weekend making phone calls to those trustees who might be persuaded.

Alejandro arrived in his new sports car, unsure what Spencer might want from him. But if Spencer had some insight into what went on at the sauna he could perhaps be useful. The two men sat in Spencer's office, sipping Earl Grey tea, although both of them would have preferred coffee.

'I know we haven't always seen eye to eye,' said Spencer, 'but I think we are both committed to seeing the work of the Trust continue. I know you weren't always happy with Pomfrey's ways of doing things. Together we could set it on a new path.'

'Yes,' said Alejandro complacently. 'I am the obvious person to take over.' He paused, sipping his tea unenthusiastically. 'I suspect there are underlying problems I may not be aware of?'

Spencer sighed. 'Yes,' he said, 'Pomfrey did make some dubious decisions. I think he might have invested some of our reserves in businesses we should not be associated with.'

'Such as?'

'The Spartacus sauna.' Spencer had the politician's art of sounding more trustworthy the further he strayed from the truth.

'Of course,' he continued, 'it has been an invaluable site for research purposes. But maybe not the wisest place in which to invest.'

Alejandro stood up and walked to the window, thinking how he might make use of this information. 'Does this mean,' he said slowly, 'that Pomfrey might have been involved in other activities at the sauna?'

'Other activities?' Spencer looked a little taken aback.

'Drugs; illicit drugs.' Alejandro turned and pointed his finger at Spencer. 'A filthy, life-destroying trade that Pomfrey was part of.' He took a deep breath. 'And now people are snooping round, asking questions about that night. We need to put an end to this.'

Spencer nodded. 'Joe agrees,' he said. 'We're just not sure what they know.'

'Sylvie and her friend think Pomfrey was murdered,' said Alejandro. 'Do you?'

'Of course not. He died of a heart attack—you signed the certificate.'

'Heart attacks can be triggered,' said Alejandro. 'You were at the sauna, you saw him.'

'I believe you were there as well,' said Spencer. 'Seems both of us could come under suspicion. Did you—?'

'Of course not.' Alejandro's voice got louder. 'How dare you suggest ... If anyone had a chance to kill Pomfrey it was you and Joe. How do I know what happened before I saw the body at his house?'

They glared at each other. 'Look,' said Spencer, 'this is ridiculous. Maybe he was killed, maybe he just had a massive heart attack. What we need is to stop people talking and move on. We don't want questions about moving the body to his house—and you don't want people questioning your certification.'

Alejandro nodded. 'But if the sauna is being used to push drugs—'

'That,' said Spencer confidently, 'is why we can count on Joe to be helpful in persuading the girls to drop it. Leave him to me.' He stood up, ready to shake Alejandro's hand. 'I'll make some calls now,' he said, 'see if we can ensure that you become the next chair of the Global AIDS Trust.' Now, he thought, he had sufficient leverage to ensure Alejandro would be a pliable chair. His dislike of Pomfrey meant he would happily accept the idea that the Trust's involvement with Spartacus had been Pomfrey's idea alone.

26

Sylvie came out of the tube and walked down Braganza Street towards the turnoff to her building. It was a Friday evening and in the distance she could hear the faint sound of sacred music, probably from St Agnes Church where she had once attended an organ concert. The streets were quiet now, the weekend rush having slowly ebbed into preparation for the week ahead.

As Sylvie adjusted her briefcase, for she was still finalising spread sheets from the Conference, she felt a sudden twinge in her back and an onset of giddiness. She felt puzzled, then a sense of slipping ... unconscious she collapsed onto the footpath. It was not until the following morning that she awoke, sore and confused, in the emergency ward at St Thomas Hospital. She was conscious of thirst, a slight headache and a strange tightness around her chest, where she could feel wads of bandaging.

'You're awake?' A nurse, large and strangely red-faced loomed over her, gradually shrinking to a more human shape.

'You've had a lucky recovery.' She handed Sylvie a glass of water. 'We had some problems tracking down your family,' she said. 'Your sister was here—she had to go home to the kids, but she'll be back soon. And we found a work colleague.'

Sylvie tried to sit up, spilling some of the water. 'What happened?' she croaked, looking around. She was in a narrow hospital bed in a small room, a chair beside her and a small window looking out over the Thames.

'You were stabbed,' said the nurse. 'Someone passing by found you and put you in a taxi to the hospital—not sure why they didn't call an ambulance. Whoever it was seems to have vanished. The police will want to question you.'

'I don't understand,' said Sylvie. 'Was I attacked?'

The nurse stood back as a young man, his stethoscope proclaiming his status, entered the room. 'Michael Groves,' he said, as if they had just met at a cocktail party. 'Glad to see you're awake. No serious injuries, loss of blood, major bruising and some damage to the left scapula. You might have a scar to remind you.'

He bent over, checking the bandages. 'Slight concussion, we'll keep you here another day or so just to make sure.'

Sylvie swallowed, struggling to think what to ask. 'Doctor,' she said, 'what happened?'

'I'd say someone tried to do some serious damage with a knife. That's all we know—apparently a taxi driver brought you into emergency last night.'

The door to her room opened again and another nurse came in, carrying a bunch of flowers. 'These were just delivered,' she said, looking at the card: *Get well, all best, from Spencer.*

'That's the colleague we contacted,' said the first nurse. 'We asked who else we should notify, but we'd already tracked down your sister.'

'My phone,' said Sylvie, looking at the small stack of her belongings placed beside the bed. 'Can I have it please?'

The nurse handed it to her, smoothing down the sheets. 'I'll get you some breakfast,' she said. 'But remember, you need to rest.'

Sylvie tried to stretch her left arm, but it was partly blocked by her bandages. Cradling her phone she called Caitlin. Shocked, Caitlin promised to come to the hospital as soon as possible, but before she could get there Sylvie's sister burst in, carrying magazines and chocolates.

'Thank God you're okay!' she cried, 'we were so worried—do

you know who attacked you? Was it a mugging? Did they take anything?'

Sylvie was about to answer when the door opened again, and two police walked in. They introduced themselves—Inspector Carolyn D'Cruz and Sergeant Edward Hunter—and assured Sylvie they would be brief. The room was now crowded, and her sister withdrew to the edge by the window.

'Just tell us exactly what you remember,' said the Inspector, the sergeant dutifully taking out a notebook. 'Do you know what time and exactly where you were attacked?'

'Probably a little before nine; I remember the sky was already getting dark. I was walking down Braganza Street—I think I must have just crossed over Gaza Street—that's all I remember ... They tell me I was brought here in a taxi?'

The sergeant looked a little puzzled by these street names but noted them correctly. The Inspector nodded.

'Apparently,' she said. 'We have located the driver. All he can tell us is that he was flagged down by a woman who helped put you into the cab and then disappeared, not leaving a name. The driver came straight to St Thomas, we've checked, and his story holds up.' She paused. 'Do you know anyone,' she asked carefully, 'who might have wanted to harm you?'

'No,' said Sylvie. 'At least—no.' She shook her head determinedly. 'No, it's all crazy.'

'That must be it,' put in her sister. 'Some crazy person, just a random attack. There are people like that.'

'If you think of anyone,' said the Inspector, 'let us know. Obviously we take an attack like this very seriously.'

But of course, as she confided with Caitlin after the police had left, there might be people who wanted to harm her. The police left, having made note of her home address, and her sister followed, in a trail of anxiety and promises to stay close.

'You've clearly scared someone,' said Caitlin, once she'd heard what happened. 'Whoever killed Pomfrey thinks you know too much. Noel had a couple of lucky escapes—but you've ended up in hospital, and who knows when he'll try again. Maybe we need to let it go—tell the police. It's too serious for us to handle on our own.'

'But what can we tell the police?' Sylvie sank back on the bed, conscious of a dull ache across her back. 'I'm scared Caitlin. But I don't know what we can do. As long as Mary insists Pomfrey died at home, and she has Alejandro to back her up, we have nothing the police could act on.'

The two women looked at each other, suddenly frightened. What might have seemed an accident when Noel claimed to have been attacked was suddenly real, underlined by the hospital bed and the heavy bandages across Sylvie's shoulder.

'Noel always said Joe was behind the attacks on him,' said Caitlin. 'Perhaps if we let him know we've dropped the investigation the attacks will stop?'

'And how do we do that?'

'Noel could ask his friend—I could ask Rahid.' She stopped, unsure. 'That is, if you agree he's not mixed up in it already.'

'It always gets back to the sauna, doesn't it,' said Sylvie wearily. 'Joe, Rahid, Alejandro, maybe Spencer … even Noel's friend, Winston.'

The nurse appeared again and checked Sylvie's temperature. 'Lunch soon,' she said, looking meaningfully at Caitlin. 'Then rest. We might let you go home tomorrow.'

Caitlin nodded. 'Maybe I can visit Noel in his shop after work,' she said, blowing an air kiss as she left the room. Sylvie sighed, hit by waves of fatigue.

News of the attack on Sylvie spread quickly. Spencer, who had been contacted by the hospital, immediately told Alejandro, leading them to speculate whether Joe might have been involved. Caitlin planned to meet up with Noel that evening and to ring Rahid afterwards. Meanwhile Mary, reading her morning copy of *The Times*, came across a small item about an attack on a young woman in Kennington, now believed to be recovering satisfactorily in hospital. Even before Spencer rang, she was convinced it was Sylvie.

Noel slumped back against the counter, knocking over a small pile of PG Wodehouse. 'Poor Sylvie,' he said. 'At least you'll believe me when I said I was being attacked. We have to go to the police.'

Caitlin sighed and explained why they had nothing concrete to tell the police. 'Do you think Joe is behind these attacks?' she asked. 'Can we get him to stop?'

'He came to the shop,' said Noel. 'He warned me. But why would he attack Sylvie?'

'She had been talking to Spencer. He and Joe might be in touch?'

Noel tried to recall exactly what Joe had said to him. 'I wonder,' he said, 'if it isn't someone working for Joe, maybe someone we don't know.'

'Like your mate Winston? Or Rahid?'

'Winston doesn't know Sylvie. But Rahid does—we had dinner together at your place. And he has history with Pomfrey'

He stood up and put the shut sign on the door. 'Let's go,' he said to Caitlin. 'Let's go and talk to Rahid. You know where he lives, don't you?'

'Yes, but—we can't just show up there—'

'Sylvie is in hospital, and I've been attacked twice. I don't think this is the time for social etiquette. I want to catch him unaware, before he can work out a story with Joe.'

The tube was crowded with early evening commuters, and they barely spoke on the trip to Paddington, each rehearsing the events of the past few weeks in their heads. Caitlin had rejected any suggestion that Rahid could be involved, but she knew he had hated Pomfrey and seemed uneasy at any mention of Joe. Noel felt angry, confused and guilty; had he not started asking questions about Pomfrey's death Sylvie would not now be lying in hospital. The decision to visit Rahid had seemed right at the time; now, trapped in a crowded underground carriage, he was less certain. Had either of them said let's not do this the other would have been relieved; as neither did they alighted together above ground at Paddington, making their way through the crowds to the Praed Street exit.

Silently they crossed Norfolk Square, Caitlin trying to remember which of the row of off-white terraces included Rahid's flat. She peered at the names stuck up by the entrance buzzer and reluctantly pushed it.

There was a long pause, during which Caitlin wished he would not be at home, then the buzzer sounded, and they walked down a narrow passageway to the back of the building. Rahid stood in the open doorway and nodded at them.

'Well,' he said, 'this is a surprise.'

'Sylvie's in hospital,' said Noel abruptly. 'But I'm assuming you knew that?'

Rahid shook his head. 'No. How would I?'

'She was attacked—' Caitlin looked at him. 'Maybe we could come in?'

Rahid nodded and led them into the small living area of the flat, cluttered with electronics and books. He pointed them to a slightly tattered beige sofa and sat cross-legged on the floor facing them.

'She was attacked last night in Kennington, probably round 9 o'clock,' said Noel. 'Where were you?'

'Working mate. At the sauna. Which as you know is a fair trot from Kennington.'

'Was Joe there?'

'Guess so. I don't leave the massage room very much when I have clients.' He stretched, cracking his hands behind his head. 'You trying to pin the blame on us are you Noel? All part of your fantasies about how Professor Lister was offed because you hate the idea he was in the sauna looking for other blokes.'

The two men glared at each other.

'It's not just a fantasy, Rahid,' said Caitlin. 'Noel was attacked, now Sylvie. Someone is trying to shut us up.'

'Well, it's not me. Like I said, I was in the sauna yesterday evening. I wouldn't even know where to find Sylvie.'

'But Joe would,' said Noel urgently. 'It wouldn't be that hard to find out. After all, he found me in the shop easily enough. Do you really think he's not mixed up in this?'

Rahid stood, knocked aside a stack of books on an old armchair and sat. 'I don't know,' he said softly. 'I know he's pretty pissed off with all this snooping around and asking questions.'

'We're stopping that,' said Caitlin. 'Can you let him know?'

She looked at Noel, who nodded, reluctantly.

'Good,' said Rahid. 'Guess you'll be off now.'

They stood up, and Caitlin held out her arms to Rahid. 'Sorry,' she said softly, 'I'm sorry if it seems we don't trust you. But it's become pretty scary.'

Rahid turned away and led them to the door. 'Take care,' he said, but in a tone that Noel heard as a warning and Caitlin as concern.

As soon as they were out of earshot, Noel turned on Caitlin. 'Why did you say we're giving up?' he demanded. 'Isn't there more reason to find out who's behind this?'

'We want Rahid to call off Joe—if it is Joe. Meanwhile we need something concrete to take to the police.'

27

On the Sunday Sylvie was discharged and her sister drove her home in a flurry of concern and promises to check in on her regularly. She decided to ignore any of the papers she had brought home with her and tidy the flat, maybe enjoy the catharsis of throwing away things she no longer needed. She was surprised at how much she had accumulated in the two years she'd lived in the flat and how few memories of the past seemed worth keeping. She seized a box of letters and photos from above the wardrobe and started culling ferociously, puzzling over mementos from several former boyfriends, one of whose names she struggled to recall. With some pleasure she discarded a few postcards that Geoffrey had sent her at the beginning of their affair. Knowing he was on holiday with his family in Mauritius had seemed bitter-sweet at the time; now she wondered why she had tolerated him.

Caitlin rang and said she would drop in after tennis—and after talking to Alejandro. She was rostered to play in a mixed doubles match, which lasted longer than she had planned, and she managed to catch Alejandro as he was about to leave. He was in a relatively good mood, having won two of his three matches, and he looked, Caitlin thought, genuinely upset at the news. Alejandro decided it best not to mention he had already been told of the attack by Spencer.

'Attacked? With a knife? I know that Kennington isn't the best neighbourhood, but who would have expected something like this? And coming so soon after the memorial for Pomfrey ...' He looked at his watch. 'Goodness,' he said, 'I have to go. Let me know how she is.'

As he walked off towards the car park Caitlin wondered how he knew Sylvie lived in Kennington, and that she had been attacked there.

Spencer, he had told Alejandro, would spend the day on the phone calling the Trustees. It was, on the whole, a frustrating few hours, involving wrong numbers, unavailable responders and polite avoidance. By late afternoon he had a strong sense that something had been decided, from which he was being deliberately excluded.

ᘓ

Normally Noel wouldn't be in the shop on Sunday, but he'd missed the usual stamp and book fair and decided he would make up for it by opening up for a few hours in the afternoon. For the first hour hardly anyone came in, which suited him, but there was a sudden flurry of customers half-way through the afternoon, and he spent some time leafing through a stack of books brought in by an older man, clearly apologetic at selling off his library, and overly optimistic about its value. He fobbed him off with two remainders, runners up from the previous year's Bannerman Prize.

He was thinking of closing the shop when there was a timid knock on the door, which was only half open, and Winston appeared.

'Hey,' said Noel, uncertain how he felt at seeing him. 'Thought you were staying in Brighton for the weekend?'

Winston shrugged. 'Came up Friday,' he said. 'On my way back this evening—thought I should look you up.'

'It's been a pretty tough weekend. My friend Sylvie got attacked—she only came out of hospital this morning.'

Winston came over and gave him a tentative hug. 'Sorry matey,' he said. 'You reckon it's the same person as did you? Couldn't it just be a random mugging?'

Noel looked at him, suddenly angry. 'Why do you keep trying to deny what's happening? Are you covering for Joe?'

Winston shook his head determinedly. 'Look,' he said 'You're a nice guy. I like you, not sure if that means anything, but I don't want you to get hurt. People like us Noel—we're the ones who get slammed when there's trouble.'

'You're still working for Joe, right? This is him warning us off.'

'I don't know, mate. Honest.' Winston put his arms around Noel and hugged him hard. 'Just wanted to let you know that I'll be back in town Thursday to see my mum, if you wanted to get together?'

Noel nodded. 'Yes,' he said, 'I'd like that. We could go to the pub for dinner?'

'Only casual, mind. When this is over let's see what happens. Now I've got to get the train back down to Brighton.'

He gave Noel a quick kiss, which hovered between friendship and lust, and left.

What, wondered Noel, did Winston mean by *when this is over*? Why travel half-way across London for a five-minute chat, which could well have been done over the phone? Still puzzling about the visit, he walked over and shut the shop door, pulling down some of the shutters. He liked being alone in the shop in the half-light that came through the bottom half of the window, it was his sanctuary. The shop would stay closed now till Tuesday; tomorrow he would ask Sylvie if she wanted a visit.

og

Noel walked down Braganza Street from the tube, wondering exactly where Sylvie had been attacked. The lift at her building was, predictably, out of order and he climbed the stairs, slightly breathless. Sylvie, when she opened the door, seemed paler than usual with the outline of a bandage visible through her light pullover.

Noel handed her one of the rather tasteless biscuits he'd bought at a convenience store after leaving the tube station. 'I should have brought flowers,' he said apologetically, 'or maybe grapes.'

Sylvie grimaced. 'No,' she said, 'I think I've had enough of being an invalid. My shoulder is still sore, but it seems there is no real damage.'

'I'm scared,' said Noel. 'Someone is out to get us.'

Sylvie nodded, holding in tears. Noel noticed that she was shaking, and tentatively put his arms around her.

'I'll be okay,' said Sylvie, sniffling. 'At least the police are onto it now.' She sighed. 'Let's not talk about it anymore. Tell me about Brighton—you still seeing that bloke, Winston?'

'I'm not sure.' But Noel felt a need to talk, and started recounting his trips to Brighton, his encounters with Joe, the welcome he'd found at *The Brigadoon* and the play reading for *The Importance of Being Earnest* where Maurice prided himself on playing Miss Prism—

He stopped. 'Sylvie,' he said, 'when you were attacked—it was a woman who reported it? And then disappeared?'

Sylvie nodded.

'What if it wasn't a woman? What if it was a man in drag who attacked you and then flagged down the cab?'

'But why would someone do that?'

'Just think, Sylvie. If someone was following you and didn't want to be recognised. All the cab driver knows is that he was flagged down by a woman who wouldn't give her name and disappeared. Didn't the cops think that was suspicious?'

'They assumed she didn't want to get involved, that's all.'

'It was dusk?—the driver would hardly have seen her? Did she speak to him?'

'I don't know. I don't think so. But can you really imagine any of the men we've been talking about disguising themselves as a woman and walking around the streets?'

'He wouldn't need to be walking if he followed you in a car. Remember I was attacked by someone in a car. Suppose he was following you and only got out to knife you? We need to find the cab driver and ask him about the woman who called him.'

Sylvie looked sceptical. 'But the police have already talked to him, and he couldn't give them any description. And how would we go about finding a cab driver? I was lucky there was one close at hand. I think Caitlin is right—we should stop doing this before one of us gets seriously hurt.'

Reluctantly Noel agreed, and the conversation moved on to the problem of finding reliable boyfriends, something they had in common. But travelling home on the tube Noel kept brooding over the way both he and Sylvie had been attacked, and whether the same person had been involved. He thought of going out, but instead settled in for an evening of television—he had a slightly embarrassed liking for *Buffy the Vampire Slayer*—and went to bed. He was already half asleep when he was suddenly struck by an idea and sat bolt upright. 'Yes!' he exclaimed, 'That's it!' Tomorrow he would call Caitlin and see if they could all get together again.

CB

Noel was not the only person to have a disturbed night.

After his failure to contact the Trustees, Spencer sensed that his control over the Trust was threatened and that even Pomfrey's death might not be enough to hide his investments in Spartacus. Sylvie had irritated him with her questions, even more so when he realised she was speaking with Elvira. His plan to install Alejandro seemed to be slipping, as none of the Trustees were prepared to give him a straight answer, and Elvira was clearly planning something. He avoided the office on Monday, planning to take Arabella for lunch to a new and glamorous restaurant in Maidenhead, where he might warn her that there could be some problems ahead, but Arabella had recently joined a hot yoga group and showed little interest in missing a session for a gourmet meal.

Alejandro, meanwhile, was worried about his son, who was still in the rehab centre but seemed to have sunk into permanent lethargy, refusing to take part in group activities and disregarding his therapist. That, and the logistics of planning human trials for his vaccine, meant he almost forgot about Sylvie and the implications of the attack on her. He had been invited to appear on a popular late night television program to explain retroviruses—'in terms our listeners can understand, most of them wouldn't make it into grammar school'—and he was struggling to find the words.

Rahid had told Joe about the attack on Sylvie, to which Joe had just grunted. He was preoccupied with the fall-off in patronage, perhaps due to the persistently warm weather, which took men out into the pubs and parks and made the heat of a sauna less enticing. He worried that further questions about Pomfrey's death could reach his investors, or the press, and that could kill the whole business.

Joe could usually sleep through anything, but Nell had returned after a few days away, demanding that he commit to the relationship, and he found himself wavering, torn between lust and boredom.

Rahid spent a restless night, waking every few hours in what he knew was a vain hope that Justin had finally come home. Moreover, the attack on Sylvie had upset him more than he'd admitted, partly because he suspected that Joe might have been involved.

At home in Highgate Mary had telephoned Spencer to check that the woman attacked was Sylvie, but he had been unusually brusque and only said he believed that she had been discharged and would take a few days off. She worried about Sylvie, but she felt unable to pick up the phone and ring her. Instead she roamed the house, determined to clear out clutter but succeeding only in moving it from one room to another. Spencer had made clear that her charity was in financial trouble, and she needed to do some serious fundraising, but the thought paralysed her, and her list of potential donors seemed pathetically small.

28

'Can we include Rahid?' Caitlin was thrilled to hear from Noel, and already planning their meeting.

Noel thought for a minute. 'Yes,' he said reluctantly, 'I don't trust him, but I don't think he's our culprit.'

'I'm not sure if Elvira is still in London. I think she was going home after the memorial.'

Elvira was planning to leave the next day and was somewhat annoyed that Spencer was not in the office. The telephone would have to do; it was a short conversation. The Trustees, she said, had decided that she should become chair and the organisation would move to Oslo, where she would hire a new manager, whose first job would be a complete forensic audit of the Trust's finances. They were, of course, extremely grateful to Spencer for his work and knew he would cooperate fully with the move, which would inevitably mean some downsizing of the Trust's activities. The Trustees were particularly concerned to end undisclosed cooperation with other agencies, such as *God Loves Us All*, which she knew accorded with Spencer's wishes.

ଔ

Noel, Caitlin and Rahid agreed to meet that evening in Sylvie's flat, Caitlin having promised to bring food because Sylvie still needed to be looked after. Noel was held up by a delay on the northern line, leaving the others to wonder why he was so insistent they meet, and Caitlin bothered that the food was getting cold.

'Sorry, sorry,' said Noel, slightly breathless after running from the tube. 'But I think I've figured it out.'

The others looked at him expectantly as Caitlin served large helpings of pasta, having raided Sylvie's cupboards to find enough plates.

'It's the other way round,' said Noel. 'It came to me: why could Pomfrey not have been killed by a woman disguised as a man?'

'In the sauna?' Sylvie sounded even more doubtful. 'How would a woman get in there?'

'It was leather night.' Noel looked at Rahid, who nodded. 'And Winston says he saw someone in full leather gear—in the dark who could tell?'

'Yes,' said Rahid cautiously, 'it is possible. No-one looks very hard at the punters when they check in, and we do have some weird costumes wandering around on leather nights.'

'But who—?' Sylvie stopped, her fork suspended. 'Mary?'

'Think about it,' said Noel urgently. 'She arranged for the body to be brought back. She called in Alejandro to do the certificate. She arranged the cremation—'

'So there could be no autopsy,' said Caitlin. 'Of course.'

'We've had trans men in the sauna,' said Rahid. 'It would be possible for a woman to get in quite easily if she were in leather gear.'

'But why would Mary? ... Oh, I see.' Caitlin looked at Noel. 'Did she know about you and Pomfrey?'

'I didn't think so. But perhaps.'

'It's the classic motive though,' said Sylvie thoughtfully. 'A jealous wife, though that's hardly how I'd have pictured Mary. But she would certainly have hated thinking she was married to a homosexual.'

'It's a bit improbable though,' said Rahid. 'She would have had to know he was at the sauna and have insulin to hand.'

'He'd been there before, hadn't he?' asked Noel. 'Not that he'd told me. He always claimed I was the only man in his life.'

'Yes,' said Rahid, 'he'd been there before. But so had the others—Spencer, Alejandro. Odd how many apparently straight guys seem to have come through Spartacus.'

'He suspected the sauna was dealing in drugs,' said Sylvie. 'At least Spencer hinted that was the case.'

'Yes,' said Caitlin eagerly, 'as did Alejandro. I still think he might have done it—he hated Pomfrey and he seems to have been there that night, though he denies it. And a lot easier for him to wander round the sauna unobserved.'

There was a moment's silence as they thought about Noel's suggestion, and in unison helped themselves to more wine.

'So,' said Sylvie to Noel, 'if you're right, how do we prove it?'

'I've thought about that. The one person we know saw the probable killer was Winston—he described someone in leather, didn't really see their face. But if we could get him to see Mary he might recognise her.'

Caitlin stood up to serve more pasta. 'The one thing you can't disguise,' she said, 'is your height. Mary and Alejandro would be about the same height, yes? But shorter than Joe or Spencer.'

'And how one walks.' Sylvie was suddenly excited by the idea. 'If Winston saw Mary from behind that might trigger a memory.'

'Of course,' said Rahid, 'it would be best if he could see them both—Mary and Alejandro.' He stared at Noel. 'So you're still seeing Winston?'

'Yes,' said Noel. 'At least, I think I am. He turns up, then he vanishes—but he seems to be in London pretty regularly. Said he'd be back Thursday—guess he'll come meet me at the shop.'

Sylvie thought. 'If I could meet Mary somewhere in the neighbourhood for a drink after work, maybe you and Winston could walk by? See if it triggers his memory?'

'As long as you don't warn him,' said Caitlin. 'Otherwise, he'll say it's her just to make you happy.'

Losing, Spencer liked to say, was not an option. Elvira's phone call had shaken him, but he thought he still had one more move. As a last resort he decided to appeal directly to the Baroness. Their one meeting had been difficult—she referred to him as the hired help and made clear she would speak only with Pomfrey—but Spencer had a strong belief in his ability to charm women.

But not, it seemed the Baroness. After several attempts to explain who he was, although she knew perfectly well as soon as he rang, she acknowledged him. 'Of course,' she said, 'the American. Still wearing those ridiculous bow ties?'

The Baroness expressed her condolences at Pomfrey's death and demanded to know if the Trust would now be wound up.

'I suppose you'll be after more of my money. But isn't this AIDS thing more or less over? You have drugs that work, don't you?'

Spencer acknowledged that yes, there were effective treatments, though no real cure. But, he stressed, HIV continued to spread rapidly in poorer parts of the world, especially among young women in Africa.

The Baroness grunted. 'That's where Pomfrey's wife has been working, yes? Always struck me as too much of a do-gooder. I liked Pomfrey because there was none of that false middle-class moralising about him. Anyway, there are lots of other ways of spending my money. That lovely Bill Gates called me last week about malaria.'

Spencer gulped. 'But surely,' he said, a little overawed, 'we owe it to Pomfrey's memory to keep the Trust thriving.'

The Baroness laughed. 'His memory? But he was planning to scale it back, now Gates and others have set up their own Fund. You might need to think about finding another organisation to mismanage.'

'We've just managed a remarkably successful Conference,' said Spencer, a little acerbically.

'Always good to go out on a high,' said the Baroness. 'Good luck.'

She put down the phone, leaving Spencer uncharacteristically flustered. The reference to *mismanagement* was particularly worrying. He hoped the Baroness was not planning to ask for details as to how her funds had been invested. All the more reason to make sure that any connection between the Trust and Spartacus sauna was firmly linked to Pomfrey rather than to him. He tried to remember if Pomfrey had ever quizzed him on the Trust's investments, and if so whether he might have shared that information. The most likely person, he reflected was Sylvie; she was clearly a problem. He suspected that Pomfrey had confided in her and he had an uneasy memory of one conversation when Pomfrey had hinted his position would need to be reassessed after the Conference. At the time he had disregarded it, but maybe this explained the dismissive attitude of the Baroness. Suddenly his options seemed very limited.

29

Sylvie felt reluctant to approach Mary, but early the next morning Mary rang, very solicitous about her health and deeply apologetic for not having been in touch.

'I just heard,' she said, not saying from whom. 'Are you alright? Do you need anything?'

'I'm almost fully recovered. It would be nice to see you,' remarked Sylvie. 'I'm back at work Wednesday. Maybe we could have a drink afterwards? In that bar we once went to in Camden Town?'

A pause. 'Alright,' said Mary uncertainly, 'if that's what you would like.'

They both knew the bar was close to Noel's shop. This discomforted Mary, but she could think of no convenient excuse to avoid it, and she agreed. Sylvie went late into the office and was relieved that Spencer was clearly preoccupied and uninterested in talking. He asked after her dutifully, then retreated to his office to make a series of phone calls.

The bar itself was a strange mix of London pub and American cocktail lounge, dimly lit with bare brick walls adorned with blown-up photographs of jazz musicians, a long bar alongside one wall beneath a dazzling array of bottles, and two rows of booths, furnished with plush dark brown seats. Sylvie chose a booth towards the back and sat waiting, nervously sipping a gin. It was time for both Mary and the boys to turn up.

A somewhat dishevelled Mary came into the bar, looked round and came over. She gave Sylvie a quick kiss, then collapsed onto the seat.

'My dear,' she said, 'I am so sorry. It must have been so awful for you.'

'I don't remember much of what happened. The doctors said I was very lucky, a nasty superficial wound and shock.'

'I was always worried for you. Living in such a rough part of town.'

Sylvie looked sceptical. 'I don't think we can blame Kennington for my attack.'

Mary stood up. 'Let me buy you a drink?'

She walked over to the bar, watched by Sylvie. This would be the perfect time for Noel to walk in with Winston, for them to catch a glimpse of Mary from behind. But there was no sign of him and Noel.

Noel was outside, pacing up and down, worried that Winston had not shown. He had seen Mary arrive, now he could see her at the bar, waiting to be served. The barman was taking his time, but then he turned to Mary and Noel realised she would soon be seated again. Where the fuck was Winston?

'Have you decided what you're going to do now?' asked Mary, carefully placing the drinks on the wooden table between them, willing her hands not to shake.

Sylvie sighed. 'I have to stay to finish off the Conference acquittals. After that I think I need a long holiday. And you?'

Mary looked down at the table. 'I don't know,' she said softly. 'It's strange—Pomfrey didn't support my mission. But now he's dead I am not sure I have the energy to carry on.'

Sylvie looked around the bar: where were Noel and Winston? Outside Noel was becoming more agitated as he saw a line of pedestrians emerging from the tube, but no sign of Winston.

'I'm so sorry for everything,' said Mary tearfully. 'I didn't want it to be like this.' She carefully put down her untouched glass. 'Maybe I should go.'

Noel was torn between watching the street and trying to see inside the bar; when he saw Mary put down her glass he panicked. Almost without thinking he walked into the bar and made for the table where the two women were seated. Sylvie's back was to him, but Mary saw him enter and froze, half-standing, as she realised who he was.

'Hello Sylvie,' said Noel calmly, 'don't you think you should introduce us?'

'I know who you are,' said Mary flatly. 'I don't need to meet you.'

'I'm surprised to see you having drinks with Sylvie after you tried to kill her.'

Mary gasped and sat back down. 'No,' she said, 'that wasn't me. I was the person who found her and called the cab. I couldn't admit that I'd been following you.'

'Why?' asked Sylvie, 'why follow me?'

'Yes,' said Mary, in a tone of utter defeat. 'Why? I wish I knew.'

'You followed me as well, didn't you?' said Noel. 'In your car. Then at the tube station.'

Mary nodded, defeated.

'So if you didn't attack me,' said Sylvie, 'who did?'

'I don't know. I was walking behind you and I think I saw a man pass you, then you seemed to totter, and you fell over. I ran over and saw you were hurt, and a cab came by. He could get you to the nearest hospital—what could I do?'

'You could have come with me.'

'Yes,' said Mary softly, 'yes, I could. I failed.' She stood up and looked directly at Noel. 'You were trying to ruin my husband and my marriage,' she said. 'I don't regret trying to hurt you.'

It was a good exit line, though she rather ruined the effect by dropping her handbag, which spilled its contents all over the floor. Scooping them up she half ran from the bar, still shaking.

Sylvie and Noel sat regarding each other for a few moments.

'Shit,' said Sylvie. 'So now we're back looking for someone else.'

'And we didn't even ask her about Pomfrey's murder.'

'I think,' said Sylvie slowly, 'we might have to get drunk.' As she stood up to go to the bar a slightly dishevelled Winston burst in.

'The train,' he said, 'stuck for twenty minutes at Three Bridges—no explanation.'

He looked at them, somewhat curious that Sylvie was there. 'So what's the problem?'

Noel sighed. 'There was someone we wanted you to meet, but she's gone. Guess it was a long shot.'

'I don't think so,' said Sylvie thoughtfully. 'She more or less admitted to attacking you. Maybe you're right about her being in the sauna.'

'Hey,' said Winston. 'Let me get a drink and then you can explain. Who are you talking about?' He turned, then looked at Sylvie. 'I'm Winston,' he said, 'but reckon you guessed that.'

'Shall we get something to eat?' asked Noel. 'Work out the next steps?'

Sylvie nodded. 'I'll call Caitlin. Maybe she'll want to join us.'

Caitlin was just contemplating a solitary meal when Sylvie rang, and she agreed to come over at once—or at least as fast as the tube would allow. Unlike Winston she was in luck; a short wait for the Circle line at Bayswater and a quick change at Kings Cross, meant she walked into the bar twenty-eight minutes later, a little flushed and expectant. The others were already eating large portions of ploughman's lunch and filled her in on what had happened.

'I've been thinking,' said Caitlin eagerly, 'How to stop these attacks. Maybe we don't have enough to tell the police but what if we go public?—at least spread it round so we scare off whoever is responsible.'

The other looked at her, unsure.

'If we start telling people that there is someone out there who is attacking people who were close to Pomfrey that will put them on their guard.'

'Do we believe Mary when she said she didn't go for Sylvie?' asked Noel. 'After all, she certainly attacked me.'

'Yes, but what would her motive be?' said Sylvie. 'She could hardly be jealous of me.'

'Why not?' Caitlin was suddenly excited. 'If she was jealous enough to go for Noel why couldn't she also have imagined you were having an affair with Pomfrey? Other people thought so.' Sylvie stared at her, not sure what to make of that comment.

'Seems to me,' said Winston, who had been largely silent since Caitlin arrived, 'that you need to have another go at the wife. You think she offed the Prof., right?'

'He's right,' said Noel. 'We should confront her head on. If she didn't do it, I'm pretty sure she knows who did.'

'Your boss, Joe,' said Sylvie, turning on Winston. 'What does he know?'

'Nothing I think.' Winston looked slightly abashed. 'He just wants you to stop asking questions which might get the sauna into trouble.'

'Spencer has called a meeting tomorrow,' said Sylvie. 'He's asked Mary and Alejandro—and me—to come to the office to discuss the future of the Trust.' She looked at Winston. 'Maybe this is the chance for you to see if you recognise anyone from that night.'

Winston nodded. 'But don't count on it,' he said. 'People look pretty different when you see them out of the sauna in their regular clothes.'

30

'Someone to see you, Spencer,' said Bronwyn, the office assistant.

Joe walked in, winked at Bronwyn and went into Spencer's office. It was his first time there, and Spencer looked uneasy to see him.

'Nice spot you have here,' said Joe, taking in the view over Russell Square.

'I have a meeting soon,' said Spencer nervously. 'This may not be the best time.'

'Never is mate,' said Joe. 'Not when it's a matter of money. The thing is,' he said, seating himself in one of the leather chairs, 'we need cash. Not a great deal, mind you—'

'Impossible.' Spencer stood up from behind his desk. 'You promised me the business would make us money.'

'And it will. We just need to build it up.'

'I've already told you I want to pull out. There's certainly no more money from here.'

'That's a problem mate.' Joe leant back, seemingly relaxed. 'If you were to withdraw your investment I'd have to explain it to the other stakeholders. I don't think they would take kindly to your lack of confidence.'

Spencer realised he needed to sound persuasive. 'I can't wait,' he said. 'I need to get my money out before there are too many questions. Which wouldn't be good for you, or for Spartacus.'

'No way.' Joe lent over towards Spencer. 'You're hardly in a position to make demands, remember. And meanwhile, can you stop that silly woman who works for you asking questions about Lister's death. It's not good for either of us.'

Meanwhile the 'silly woman' was in the outer office, waiting for Mary and Alejandro. She had alerted Noel to meet Winston at the café across the road, ready to see Mary as she arrived, and she was increasingly anxious how this might play out. Not for the first time she wondered whether they might not have concocted a massive fantasy to explain a middle-aged man having a heart attack in an inconvenient time and place. Even if Winston did recognise someone she was not certain what the next steps would be, and whether Winston's word would carry any weight.

'They're here,' said Bronwyn, opening the door to Spencer's office and showing in Mary and Alejandro. They looked startled at seeing Joe in the room, who had settled back in his chair and showed no sign of leaving. After an awkward couple of minutes, while Spencer greeted the arrivals, he signalled to Joe, who stood up slowly and left the room.

'I'll walk you out,' said Spencer, afraid Joe might linger and talk to Sylvie, who was still in the outer office. He opened the front door to the building and watched Joe walk down Southampton Row. Sylvie came into the office and busied herself arranging coffee and biscuits.

'So,' said Spencer, walking back in and taking his seat at his desk, 'I thought the four of us should meet to discuss how best to save the Trust. It is, after all, Pomfrey's legacy and I'm afraid there is a real danger of it collapsing. I fear Elvira has been plotting against us all.'

He gave them an edited version of his conversation with Elvira, omitting any reference to audits or investments, and looked at them expectantly. It was of course awkward that he had promised both Mary and Alejandro that he would support them to replace Pomfrey, but he assumed they were unlikely to have confided in each other.

'That's impossible!' Alejandro was trembling with rage. 'Surely there are legal requirements to maintain the Trust in Britain? Under our leadership?'

'I'm afraid not,' said Spencer. 'The agreement was that Pomfrey would remain chair as long as he wished, and that his succession was a matter for the Trustees. But of course—' nodding at Mary— 'one would expect the wishes of his widow and heir would be taken into consideration.'

Mary was about to say something, but Spencer continued. 'Under the circumstances I wonder whether we might propose a joint leadership shared between the two of you? I think that could be the basis for a very attractive proposal that we could put to the Trustees. They have clearly been led astray by Elvira, and this might give them the opportunity to reconsider. What do you think Sylvie?'

It was very unlikely thought Sylvie, but as she struggled to find a tactful way of saying this the door burst open and Winston and Noel came in.

'That's him!' said Winston, pointing at Spencer. 'He was the man I saw at Spartacus the night the Prof. was killed.'

'Who is this man?' asked Spencer, as they all turned to stare at Winston. 'Sylvie, do you know him?'

'Yes. But are you sure Winston?' said Sylvie. 'We thought it was Mary?'

'Nah,' said Winston, 'It's him. I saw him just now on the steps with Joe—he put his hand on Joe's back, as he was leaving. And I remembered I'd seen him come out of the cubicle where Prof. was, he made the same gesture with his hands.'

'This is absurd,' said Spencer. 'I don't know who you are, but I suggest you leave immediately.'

Winston stared at Spencer. 'I think you do know me mate,' he said slowly. 'I think we've met before, at the Spartacus Sauna.'

'Wait,' said Mary, trembling. 'Are you saying Spencer killed Pomfrey?'

'Don't know that. But I do know he was the bloke I saw at the sauna that evening.'

'And we thought it was you Mary,' said Sylvie apologetically. 'Dressed as a man.'

'Yes,' said Mary softly, 'I was there. I'd followed Pomfrey—I knew he went to sordid leather bars, so I put on his jacket and cap and followed him. But when I saw he was going into the sauna I was too frightened to go in, I went home. Then you phoned,' she said, turning to Spencer. 'You told me he had had a heart attack and we needed to get him out of there. You told me to call Alejandro and tell him Pomfrey was diabetic. You encouraged me to have a quick cremation. Why did you do that?'

'I was protecting you,' said Spencer. 'Avoiding scandal.'

'Or protecting yourself,' said Alejandro. 'Elvira warned me that you were mixed up in the sauna. With that man—Joe. You were scared Pomfrey knew you'd invested Trust funds in that business.'

'And what about you?' Spencer turned on Alejandro. 'You hated him. Get him out of the way and you'd get your own way on the vaccine trials.'

'Were you in the sauna that night?' asked Noel.

Alejandro nodded. 'Yes, early on. I dropped in to check on our survey—one of the researchers hadn't shown up. But I didn't see Pomfrey.'

'I believe you,' said Mary, looking at Winston. 'I don't know who you are, or why you saw it, but it makes sense. I just didn't want to believe he'd been killed.' She turned on Spencer. 'You bastard, Spencer. You hated him because he was a homosexual.'

'So did you Mary,' said Spencer softly, 'that's why we could work together.'

'Well, I loved him,' said Noel, close to tears. 'So many of you hated him. But at least now we know who did it.'

Spencer was standing with his back to the window. 'I'd like to see you prove it,' he said, as if dismissing a childish fantasy. 'If it hadn't been for my help there would have been a scandal you'd all have hated.'

Mary looked at him stonily. 'When you brought back his clothes the next morning,' she said, thinking, 'you didn't return his glasses. You gave them to me a few days later.'

'I must have picked them up when we found the body. Obviously in the heat of the moment I forgot to return them with the rest of his things.'

'No,' said Winston, 'I found the body. And there were no glasses. I think you must have been there and taken them away before I found him.'

'That's hardly proof,' said Spencer airily. 'Who would believe you?—a low-life sauna attendant?'

'I do,' said Mary. 'I thought *I* was responsible—that I'd driven him away and he was going to leave me.' She looked at Noel. 'That's why I attacked you,' she said. 'But it was only to scare you— I'm not a killer.'

'We can go to the police,' said Sylvie. 'There's always proof once the police start to look. Tracking the movements of your car that evening, for a start.'

Spencer looked slightly alarmed. 'I wouldn't do that,' he said. 'There are penalties for wasting the police's time.'

'Mary,' said Sylvie, 'do you think Spencer was the man you saw knife me?'

Mary looked at Spencer, as if seeing him for the first time. 'I don't know,' she said slowly, 'I couldn't swear it was him.'

Alejandro was looking increasingly alarmed, thinking of the possible publicity and questions about his willingness to provide a death certificate. 'I wonder,' he said tentatively, 'if we aren't rushing to conclusions. What hard evidence do we have, after all?'

'The insulin bottle,' said Noel. 'The vial Winston found in the cubicle.'

'Anyone could have put it there,' said Spencer defiantly.

'Insulin?' Alejandro sat forward, suddenly alert. 'That's clever— even if there'd been a post-mortem you'd told me he was diabetic, and I'd have assumed he overdosed. But you can't just wander into a pharmacy and buy it. The police can track down where the bottle came from—you still have it?'

Winston nodded.

'Spencer, you absolute bastard!' said Mary, shaking with rage. 'You told me Pomfrey had been diagnosed as diabetic and didn't want me to worry. You made sure I lied about that to everyone.'

Somehow that seemed the worst betrayal of the lot, and Mary was close to tears. She blew her nose rigorously, then seemed to regain her composure as she looked across the room at Noel. 'We won't let him get away with this,' she said, 'there are too many of us here for that to happen.'

'Did Joe know?' asked Winston. 'Is that why he packed me off that evening?'

'He called me after he found the body.' Spencer sounded more defensive, as he tried to find the best way to end the conversation. 'But this whole thing is absurd,' he shouted. 'Pomfrey died of a heart attack after over-exerting himself, you mightn't like it but that's what happened. I tried to save both Mary and the Trust embarrassment and you all turn on me with some fantastical story about murder and insulin bottles.'

'It was murder alright,' said Noel.

'And if—*if* you're right—maybe it was Joe. He didn't like Pomfrey snooping around the sauna, asking questions. I had no reason to kill Pomfrey just before the Conference, that was going to be our joint triumph.'

'Pomfrey knew too much about your misuse of Trust funds,' said Sylvie. 'And the Trustees were all coming to London for the Conference. You had to get him out of the way before he could talk to them.' She stood up and turned towards Spencer. 'I assume you attacked me because you thought I also knew that you'd been misappropriating Trust funds. The police who interviewed me after I was attacked will want to hear about this.'

Spencer lunged towards Sylvie, as if he would physically prevent her ringing the police, but found his way blocked by Mary and Noel. Sylvie went into the adjoining room and dialled.

'This is just crazy,' expostulated Spencer, but without much conviction. He looked at Alejandro as his only possible ally, but Alejandro had sunk into his chair and was calculating how to avoid further involvement.

'The Inspector asked me to come down to the station and make a statement,' said Sylvie. 'Noel, could you and Winston come with me?'

'I'll come as well,' said Mary firmly. 'He was my husband.'

'I'll just get back to the labs ...' Alejandro was already halfway out of the door, leaving Spencer alone. The others regrouped on the street, then summoned a cab to take them to the Vauxhall police station. In the taxi Mary and Noel sat apart, ignoring each other, while Sylvie made desultory conversation with Winston and wondered again whether they had imagined the whole story of Pomfrey's murder.

How strange, thought Noel, to be in a cab with the woman who had tried to kill him, but if she had loved Pomfrey maybe that excused her. Meanwhile Mary felt torn between guilt and anger, a deep sense that had she been more understanding Pomfrey would still be alive and they would have found a way of moving forward. She glanced surreptitiously at Noel, trying to imagine what his hold over Pomfrey might have been and wishing that she had tried to talk to him rather than attack him.

31

Rather reluctantly Inspector D'Cruz decided to interview Spencer at his home. By the time she arrived he had changed into more casual clothes and warned Arabella that the allegations against him were ridiculous, but he was confident they would come to nothing.

'I apologise for taking up your time,' said the Inspector, noticing the expensive and very neat décor of the large sitting room into which Spencer had led her. 'But you know that some very serious claims have been made and I need to follow up.'

'Of course, Inspector. Ask me anything.' Spencer leant back, giving the appearance of being completely relaxed, although Arabella noticed a slight twitch in his left eye.

'Where were you last Friday evening, round nine?' asked the Inspector, signalling to her sergeant to take notes.

'Last Friday: why I was here, wasn't I?' he said, turning toward Arabella. 'We held the memorial the day before, I was a little tired.'

'I think you went to the supermarket for me?' said Arabella. 'We needed that special pasta you like. And you bought some wine.' She bit her lip, restraining herself from commenting that he'd been gone a surprisingly long time.

'Yes, of course,' said Spencer, 'I did nip out for a bit. But only to do some supermarket shopping.'

'And you drove? Can you confirm that this is the number plate of your car?'

Inspector D'Cruz nodded at Sergeant Hunter who showed him an image of a number plate. She didn't think it necessary to explain that they had a dozen or so number plates from cameras in the area, and only checked them after Sylvie's accusation against Spencer.

Spencer nodded uneasily. 'Yes,' he said, 'I think that is mine.'

'My problem,' said the Inspector, 'is that a CCTV camera picked up that plate near Kennington station round about the time Sylvie was attacked. Now for someone who lives in Knightsbridge that seems rather a long way to go for pasta and wine, I think you said?'

Arabella gave an involuntary shriek, then sat back.

'There must be some mistake,' said Spencer. 'I've never been to Braganza Road—' He stopped, gulped hard.

'Now that is interesting, sir, seeing I never mentioned a street name.' She stood up. 'I think maybe we need to continue this discussion at the police station. We might ask you to submit to a police line-up.'

Spencer stood up, the perfect patrician. 'Of course, Inspector,' he said. He turned to Arabella. 'Call Ffolkes, would you please darling, that rather pushy lawyer your father trusts. Tell him I'm being taken to the police station.'

Spencer looked at the Inspector who mouthed the word Vauxhall. 'And,' he continued, 'there is a gross miscarriage of justice he should attend to.' He gave a slight smile, memories perhaps of similar events he'd seen in film. 'I'm ready, Inspector.'

At the station Spencer was questioned again, then led into a small room with four other men of similar height and made to stand against a wall. The police had decided Mary's evidence would be too biased to be of much use, but they had called back the cab driver who had picked up Sylvie, and he was quite enjoying his momentary importance. He had told the police that he had only caught a glimpse of a man walking quickly away from the girl who was lying on the footpath, but the light was still good, and the man had walked in front of his cab, so possibly he would recognise the face.

As a result of an unambiguous identification, and the evidence of the cameras, Spencer was charged with recklessly endangering Sylvie. It was touch and go whether they could get a conviction, the Inspector admitted, and unfortunately, there was not sufficient evidence to charge him with killing Pomfrey and given the absence of a body it was unlikely there could be. But, as Caitlin pointed out, his trial would allow them ample opportunity to point out that his attack on Sylvie only made sense if he had already murdered Pomfrey. Spencer had vacated the Trust offices, which would soon be taken over by a Russian shipping firm, and barely left home as he awaited the trial; Arabella spent more and more time at her mother's home in Hertfordshire and was quietly consulting a divorce lawyer.

'Remember Al Capone,' said Elvira, who was briefed by regular calls from Sylvie. 'They got him for tax evasion. You might never prove he killed Pomfrey but we have evidence he misappropriated Trust funds.'

03

After a brief trial Spencer was cleared on the charge of attacking Sylvie when the cabbie's evidence was demolished in court and the police declined to follow up on allegations of murder, even though Joe was willing to testify that Spencer had access to the sauna through the back door and seemed to have been there more often than he admitted. Had the police checked at the time they might have found the leather jacket and cap he wore, but they were long gone, weighed down with rocks in a backwater off the Ebbsfleet. The cap was in the distinctive pantone blue of Yale University, which had struck Rahid when he glanced someone wearing it, but he had failed to make the connection to Spencer.

Taking Pomfrey's glasses and dropping the insulin vial had been a silly mistake, thought Spencer, but had there been questions it would have appeared Pomfrey took an overdose by accident. Putting an amyl bottle in his hand should have made a heart attack more believable. He had been surprised how easily Mary had accepted the idea of a rapid cremation, which made an autopsy impossible.

Elvira, however, had briefed a forensic accountant who had begun discussions with the Charity Commission for England and Wales. With his marriage, career, and reputation in tatters, Spencer took refuge in drink and sleeping pills. One night, half drunk, he telephoned for a male escort, but when the man arrived he thrust fifty pounds at him and slammed the door. The evening before he was summoned to answer questions at the Commission he deliberately swallowed all the remaining pills with copious drafts of whisky and was found by a cleaning woman several days later. His funeral was small and, ironically, at the same cemetery where Pomfrey had been cremated.

Six Months Later

Sylvie walked out of her apartment in Grünerløkka and shivered; it was still half-dark and steady chills blew off the fjord. But she liked her new life in Oslo and enjoyed working with Elvira. She stayed in touch with Caitlin, who was now working more directly with Alejandro. He had accepted the flaws in his vaccine model that had bothered Pomfrey, and was optimistic he could commence human trials the following year. Rahid was now fully employed in the laboratories and had abandoned massage, while Justin had decided they should continue to see each other but live apart. After the publicity of the trial, Justin had met someone in a backroom bar who told him that Pomfrey had been known to frequent sex clubs, but always as voyeur. The Spartacus had been sold and was now doing good business as a *wellness centre* for wealthy businessmen.

Mary had come to an agreement with Oxfam to hand over those of her programs that fitted their strategy and had quietly withdrawn support for abstinence programs. She thought of volunteering for the Terrence Higgins Trust, but so far that seemed too daunting. She did, however, offer to give Noel any of Pomfrey's books that he might want as a memento, and was relieved that he seemed unlikely to accept. After several unsatisfactory evenings with Winston, Noel had started seeing someone older, staider, and, most important, unattached; they were tentatively talking of finding a flat together. Winston had moved back to London and enrolled in a course at a new Photography Institute. If it wasn't a case of them all living happily ever after, Noel, who had gone back to Brighton for the premiere of *The Importance of Being Ernest*, comforted himself with Wilde's observation that: *The good ended happily, and the bad unhappily. That is what Fiction means.*

Acknowledgements

A number of people provided ideas and sounding boards along the way: most importantly Tom Tanhchareun, with whom the plot was devised, and others who guided me in ways ranging from the search for HIV vaccines to Google maps of London. Of course, part of the joy of discussing a work in progress is the diametrically opposite advice one collects along the way. I had the benefits of a professional read from Andrew Nette, and input from a number of friends and colleagues including:

Colin Batrouney; Carolyn D'Cruz; Andrea Goldsmith; Robin Gorna; Edward Hunter; Sharon Lewin; Atari Metcalf; Christos Tsiolkas; Filip Vukasin; Simon Watney.

I drew largely on memories of time in London and Brighton, and friends in those cities may recognise some places, and forgive me those I have invented. This story reflects many years of reading detective fiction and gay history; particularly useful were Paul Burston: *Queen's Country* and Jeremy Atherton: *Gay Bar: Why We Went Out.*

And special thanks to Gordon Thompson, editor and publisher extraordinaire.

Dennis Altman

Dennis Altman has written widely on sexuality, politics and culture both in Australia and globally. He was President of the AIDS Society of Asia and the Pacific, and in 2006 *The Bulletin* named him as one of the 100 most influential Australians. He is patron of the Australian Queer Archives and the Pride Foundation.

Since his first book, *Homosexual: Oppression and Liberation*, Dennis Altman has written seventeen books, including *Global Sex* and *Unrequited Love: Diary of an Accidental Activist.*